ROSS BOLLINGER PRESENTS
Pencilmation
THE ~~GRAPHIC~~ NOVEL
GRAPHITE
#1

PENGUIN YOUNG READERS LICENSES
AN IMPRINT OF PENGUIN RANDOM HOUSE LLC, NEW YORK

FIRST PUBLISHED IN THE UNITED STATES OF AMERICA BY PENGUIN YOUNG READERS LICENSES,
AN IMPRINT OF PENGUIN RANDOM HOUSE LLC, NEW YORK, 2022

VISIT US ONLINE AT PENGUINRANDOMHOUSE.COM.

MANUFACTURED IN ITALY

ISBN 9780593383742 10 9 8 7 6 5 4 3 2 1 LEG

DESIGN BY TAYLOR ABATIELL

Pencilmate dedicates
this book to all the fans
who have laughed with him
(and at him!) over the years.

THANK YOU FOR KEEPING PENCILMATION ALIVE!

TABLE OF CONTENTS

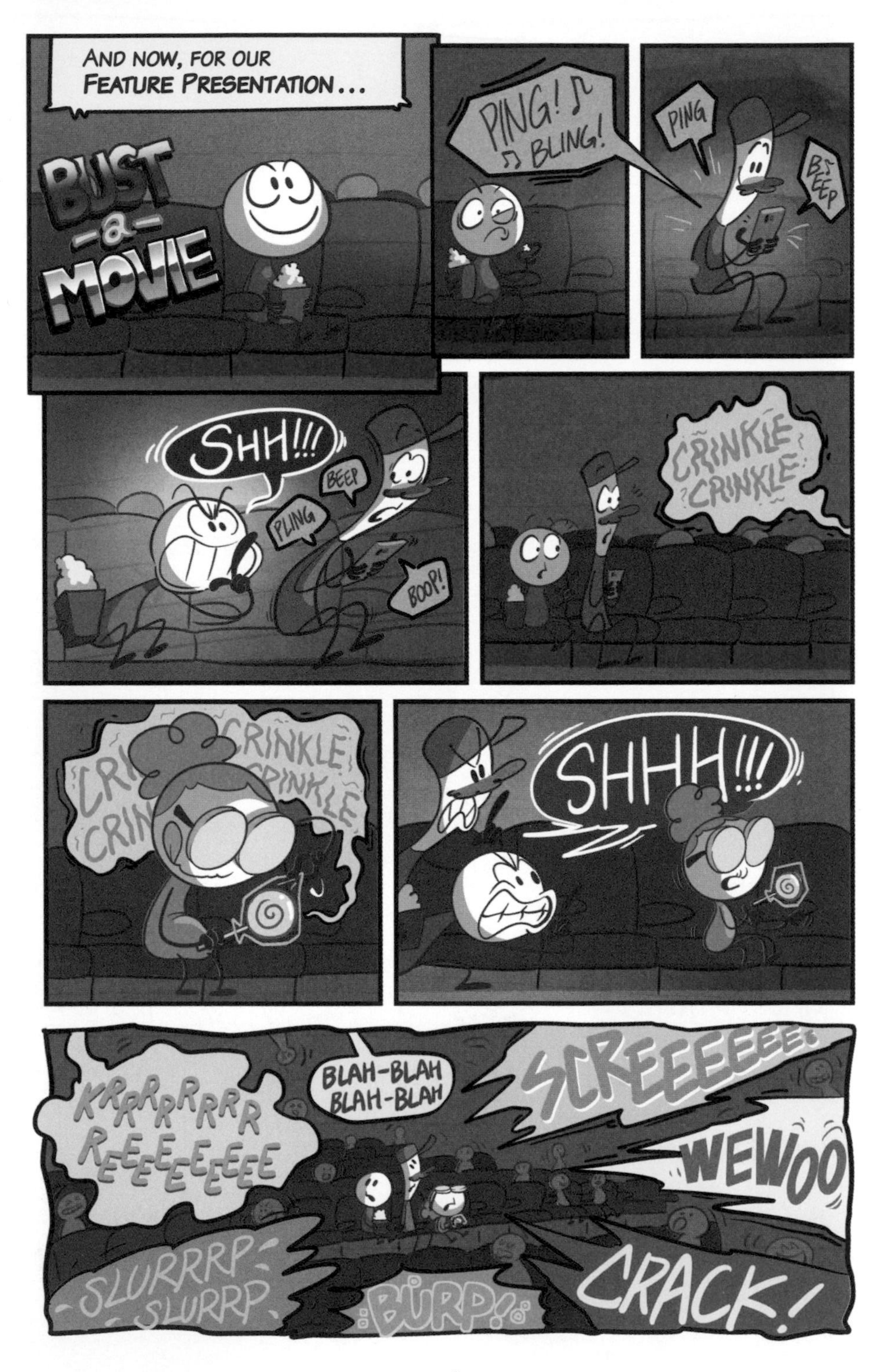
AND NOW, FOR OUR FEATURE PRESENTATION...
BUST -a- MOVIE
PING! ♪ ♫ BLING!
PING
BEEP
SHH!!!
BEEP
PLING
BOOP!
CRINKLE CRINKLE
CRINKLE CRINKLE
SHHH!!!
KRRRRRRRR REEEEEEEEE
BLAH-BLAH BLAH-BLAH
SCREEEEEE
WEWOO
SLURRRP SLURRP
BURP!
CRACK!

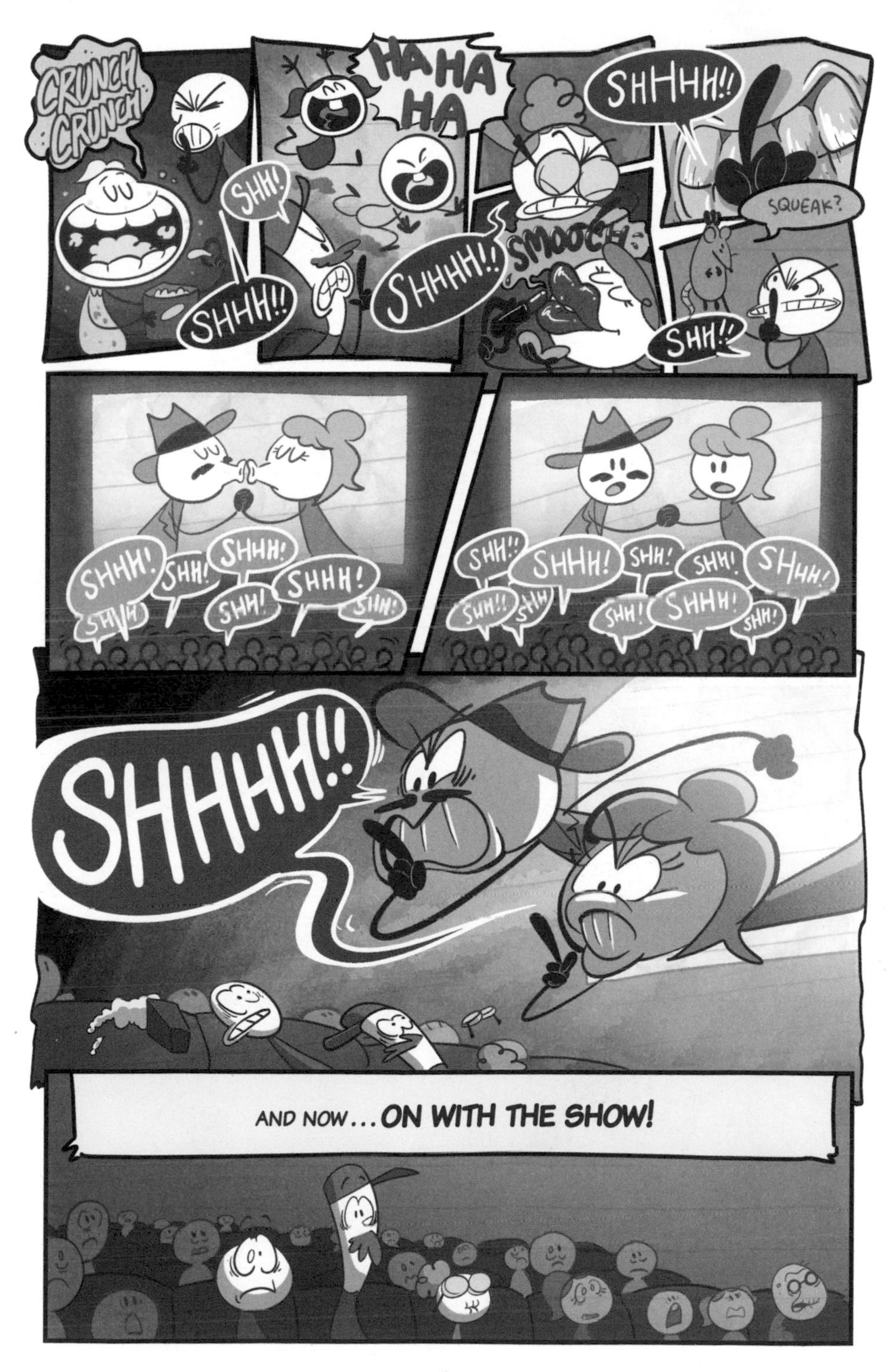

CRUNCH CRUNCH
SHH!
SHHH!!
HA HA HA
SHHHH!!
SHHHH!!
SMOOCH
SQUEAK?
SHH!!
SHHH! SHH! SHHH! SHHH! SHH! SHH!
SHH!! SHHH! SHH! SHH! SHHH! SHH!! SHH! SHHH! SHH!
SHHHH!!
AND NOW... ON WITH THE SHOW!

WHAT'S SYRUP, DOC?
IT WAS BREAKFAST TIME AT THE PENCIL PAD...
...AND OUR HERO WAS ENJOYING A MODEST MEAL.
SNARF
SNARF
BUT WHAT WAS THIS? PENCILMATE'S LITTLE BROTHER WAS IN DIRE NEED OF SOME OF THAT DELICIOUS MAPLE SYRUP!
SYRUP

ALWAYS A CARING AND ATTENTIVE OLDER SIBLING, PENCILMATE HAPPILY SHARED THE SUGARY WEALTH!
SYRUP
SYRUP
PPFFPFFFT!!
ALACK! THE DREADED FART OF AN EMPTY BOTTLE!
ALWAYS QUICK TO NOTICE HIS BROTHER'S DISTRESS, PENCILMATE SPRANG INTO ACTION!
!

He checked his Backup Supply!
He checked his Doomsday Supply!
He checked the Backup to his Backup Doomsday Supply!
...
All for naught!
Our hero had a problem...
...a problem he was determined to make right!

PENCILMATE KINDLY DRIED THE TEARS OF THE DISTRAUGHT YOUNGSTER AND FLEW OUT THE FRONT DOOR!
JIMBO MART
$$$
WITH THE FERVOR OF A BLOODHOUND ON THE HUNT, PENCILMATE SCOURED THE BREAKFAST AISLE AT THE LOCAL JIMBO MART.
/SLUG

FLIPPIN' FLAPJACKS! 'TWAS A GLORIOUS SIGHT!
MOOSE
SYRUP
MOOSE
AND ONLY ONE BOTTLE LEFT?! WHAT LUCK!
MOOSE
MOOSE
WAYLAID BY A WRINKLY RIVAL!
SYRUP
MOOSE

OUR STOIC HERO TOOK THE UNEXPECTED BLOW WITH DIGNITY AND GRACE.
BUT ALL HOPE WAS LOST...
MOOSE SYRUP
MADE IN CANADA
...OR WAS IT?
PENCILMATE PROMPTLY SET A DIRECT COURSE FOR CANADA, HOME OF ALL MAPLE SYRUP!

THROUGH HOWLING WIND AND BITING SLEET,
OUR HERO FORGED HIS PATH ACROSS A TREACHEROUS PEAK!
STUMBLING UPON A CLEARING,
HIS EYES WERE MET BY A WONDROUS VISION!
!!!
AHOY! AN OASIS OF MARVELOUS, MAPLEY GOODNESS!

HANDS TREMBLING WITH EXCITEMENT, PENCILMATE READIED HIS BOTTLE, PREPARING TO PARTAKE IN THIS GURGLING FEAST OF LIQUID RICHES!
RUMBLE
PENCILMATE REVIVED HIMSELF ONLY TO DISCOVER AN UNSPEAKABLE HORROR!
A FLEET OF SYRUP-SUCKING TRUCKS HAD DESCENDED UPON THE OASIS LIKE A HORDE OF LOCUSTS!

PARDON MY FRENCH CANADIAN, BUT THESE TRUCKS REALLY SUCKED!
SO LONG!
LATE-STAGE CAPITALISM HAD STRUCK AGAIN!
...
THE SYRUP SPRINGS HAD BEEN TOTALLY SUCKED DRY!
NOTHING WAS LEFT BUT A SINGLE DROP!

FORTUNATELY, OUR HERO WAS KNOWN FOR BEING A SMART-BRAINED THINKY GUY!
HE REASONED THAT IF A *TREE* COULD PRODUCE SYRUP, WHY COULDN'T *OTHER* OBJECTS PRODUCE SYRUP, TOO?
DOTH HE DARE TO DREAM? COULDST A HUMBLE ROCK PRODUCETH *THE DELICIOUS NECTAR* HE SO ARDENTLY SOUGHT?
CLANK!
EUREKA!!
SYRUP!

WITH THE KEY TO SYRUP EXTRACTION IN HAND, PENCILMATE *TAPPED INTO ACTION!*
SCHOOL
MEANWHILE, BACK AT HOME...

SUDDENLY THE DOOR BURST OPEN, AND FROM THE SHADOWS EMERGED A TRIUMPHANT PENCILMATE, PRECIOUS SYRUP IN TOW! *HE WAS BACK, BABY!*

PENCILMATE POPPED THE CORK OFF HIS HARD-FOUGHT BOUNTY...

AND A DELICATE BOUQUET OF SCENTS EMERGED FROM THE BOTTLE...

HE HAD INDEED COME THROUGH FOR HIS LITTLE BROTHER THIS TIME!
XX
O CURSES! O TRAGEDY! FOR WHAT HADST PENCILMATE DONE BUT IN ERROR KILLED HIS YOUNGEST OF KIN?!?

BUT WHAT WAS THIS? MINI-PENCILMATE WASN'T DEAD...
NOM
NOM
NOM
NOM
NOM
NOM
HE WAS DEAD HUNGRY!!!
MINI-PENCILMATE WAS ALIVE AND BETTER THAN EVER!
THIS CALLED FOR A CELEBRATION!
SYRUP
THE TWO PROCEEDED TO PASS BACK AND FORTH THEIR SUPPLY OF EVERYTHING SYRUP, FINALLY INDULGING TOGETHER IN THEIR DELICIOUS BREAKFAST.
AND THEY LIVED HAPPILY EVER AFTER... OR, AT LEAST, UNTIL THEIR NEXT DENTIST APPOINTMENT.
FIN.

Bored of texting the **same old friends?** Tired of the jokes you've heard **a thousand times** before? Do you wish someone interesting would **slide into your DMs?**

Then look no further . . . because what you need is an

EXTRATERRESTRIAL PEN PAL!

Sounds impossibly complex, right? Well . . . it's not! Just send us a message, and using our patented Sky-Zooka™ technology, we'll fire that sucker into the frigid vacuum of space! In moments, your missive will be in the hands of an alien life-form.

The question is . . . which one will reply to you?

BLORT

A sponge-based creature living alone on the underside of an asteroid, Blort likes passively absorbing vapors from the void and counting stars in nearby nebulae with its two thousand eyes, as well as going to brunch on Sundays.

THE ENTITY

This mysterious cloud of sentient gas has been receiving and replying to thousands of messages from Earth children for decades. Scientists have concluded that it is immensely powerful, and very lonely.

SPANGULON

When she's not leading her armies of insect-like warriors in solar-system-spanning swarms to invade and colonize new worlds, Spangulon enjoys doing yoga and collecting space stamps.

SUSAN

A pleasant middle-aged woman who is trapped in a black hole.

XFR###-973

A biomechanical organism from a distant clusterworld near Alpha Centauri, XFR###-973 is the most intelligent extraterrestrial ever encountered, with a cyber-mind capable of processing quintillions of pieces of information simultaneously. You may not even comprehend its reply!

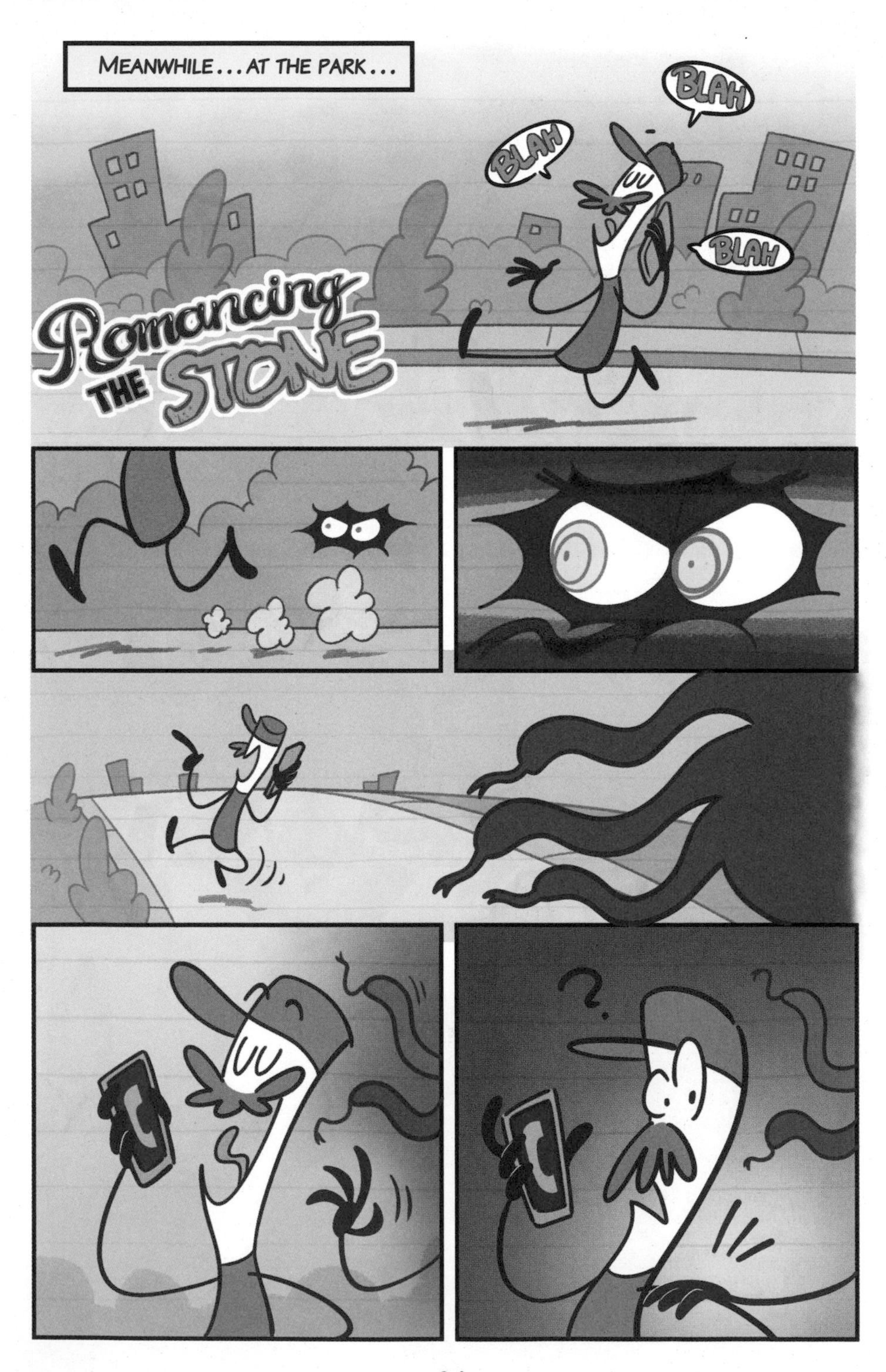
MEANWHILE... AT THE PARK...
BLAH
BLAH
BLAH
Romancing THE STONE
?

HA! HA! HA!
HA! HA! HA!
HA!
?!

HA! HA!
HA!
HA! HA!
HA! HA!
OOH... AAH...
...OOHH...
AH...
HMMMM...
HM
OOH...
AAAH...
OH...
...AAH!

!?
Fine Art
...

LATER...
GALLERY OF STONE

END

Holy Crab!
PENCILMISS
On a balmy day at the beach, Pencilmiss puts the finishing touches on her sandy masterpiece...
!!
Pencilmate, on the other hand...

WELL, AT LEAST HE'S TRYING?
!?
FLOPT
PENCILMISS GENEROUSLY OFFERS HER ASSISTANCE.
BUT PENCILMATE IS FILLED WITH TERRIBLE PRIDE AND REJECTS IT.
HE'S DETERMINED TO MAKE A SANDCASTLE ON HIS OWN!
AND SO HE KEEPS TRYING...

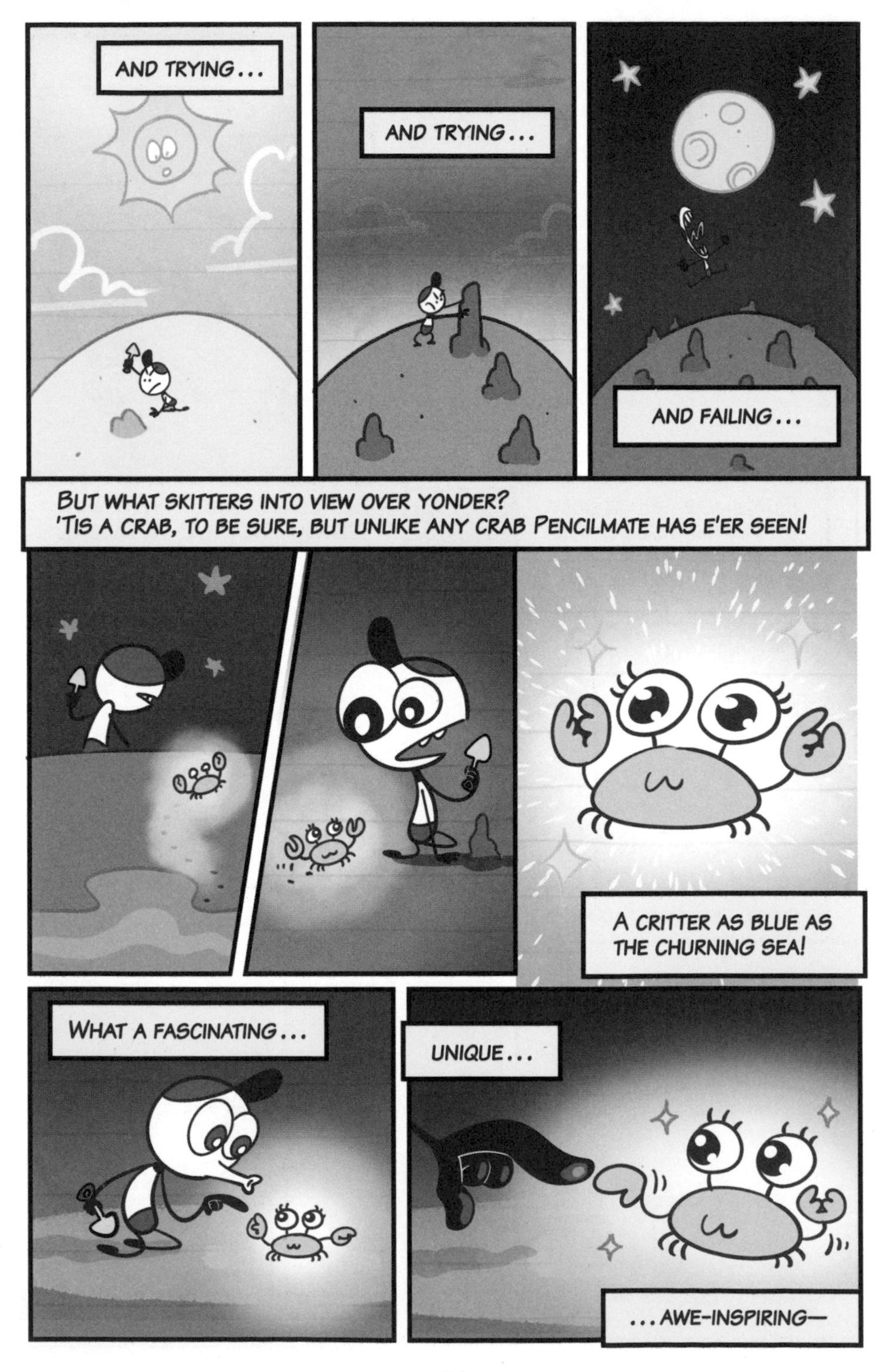
AND TRYING...
AND TRYING...
AND FAILING...
BUT WHAT SKITTERS INTO VIEW OVER YONDER?
'TIS A CRAB, TO BE SURE, BUT UNLIKE ANY CRAB PENCILMATE HAS E'ER SEEN!
A CRITTER AS BLUE AS THE CHURNING SEA!
WHAT A FASCINATING...
UNIQUE...
...AWE-INSPIRING—

YEEEEEEOOWWCH!
PINCHED BY THAT STUPID CRAB! PENCILMATE CURSES ALL THE DUMB CREATURES OF THE SEA!
LITTLE DID HE REALIZE, HOWEVER, THAT THIS IS NO ORDINARY STUPID CRAB.
STRANGE SENSATIONS COURSE THROUGH PENCILMATE'S BODY.
TREMBLE BEFORE THE ALMIGHTY ABOMINATION THAT IS...
CRABMATE!

THE NEXT MORNING AT PENCILMISS'S HOUSE...
I'M WITNESSING SOME INCREDIBLE SCENES HERE AT THE BEACH. A FREAKISHLY HUGE CRAB IS DESTROYING EVERY SANDCASTLE IN SIGHT.
NEWS
WOULDN'T IT BE TERRIBLE IF IT SMASHED THIS INCREDIBLY ELABORATE ONE OVER HERE—
PENCILMISS
!!
OH NO, HERE HE COMES!
PENCIL

ROARRR
BUT HOLD ON JUST A SECOND!
PENCILMISS IS ON THE SCENE! AND SHE'S GONNA SHOW THAT CRAB WHO'S THE SANDCASTLE BOSS!
LET THE BATTLE COMMENCE!
CRABMATE ♂
HP
PENCILMISS ♀
HP
EXP
JUMP!
TOO SLOW, YOU CLUMSY CRUSTACEAN!

These two titans are evenly matched.
Pencilmiss
!?
With raging fury, the crab demolishes Pencilmiss's master creation after all.
A tragic loss for the sandcastle community.

DAZED BUT ALIVE, PENCILMISS'S INFINITE RESILIENCE SEES HER THROUGH ANOTHER DAY.
RUMBLE...
!?
...OR PERHAPS NOT.
BUT PENCILMISS HAS ONE LAST TRICK UP HER SLEEVE...
OR RATHER, THIRTY-TWO TRICKS IN HER MOUTH!
CRUNCH!

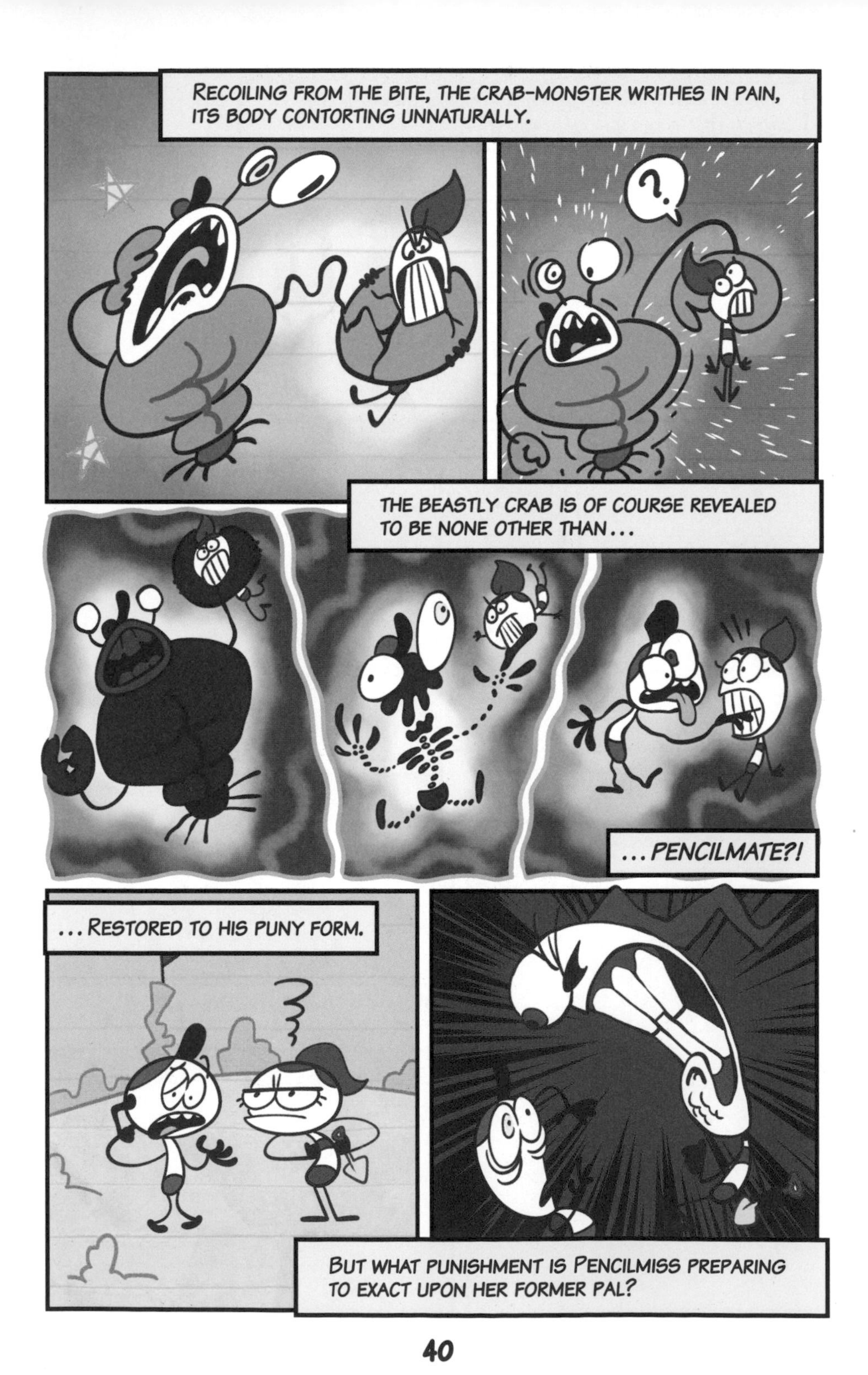
RECOILING FROM THE BITE, THE CRAB-MONSTER WRITHES IN PAIN, ITS BODY CONTORTING UNNATURALLY.
?
THE BEASTLY CRAB IS OF COURSE REVEALED TO BE NONE OTHER THAN...
...PENCILMATE?!
...RESTORED TO HIS PUNY FORM.
BUT WHAT PUNISHMENT IS PENCILMISS PREPARING TO EXACT UPON HER FORMER PAL?

SHE OFFERS HIM . . . HER PARTNERSHIP?
???
THROUGHOUT THE REST OF THE DAY AND WELL INTO THE NIGHT, PENCILMATE DISCOVERS THE POWER OF TEAMWORK . . .

PLUMP
BUT LET'S NOT UNDERESTIMATE THE POWER OF HAVING A GOOD CAPTAIN AT THE HELM.
COUGH
COUGH
HER SANDCASTLE NOW RESTORED TO ITS FORMER GLORY, PENCILMISS THANKS HER NEW FIRST MATE AND HEADS FOR HOME.

BUT WHAT'S THIS? THE MOONLIGHT STRIKES AGAIN, AND PENCILMISS'S BITE PUSHES A PINK WOOZINESS THROUGHOUT PENCILMATE'S VEINS.
WRITHING AND CONTORTING, PENCILMATE HAS TRANSFORMED INTO...
...PENCILMISS!
CAN'T A GAL GET A BREAK?!
END

RUN of the TREADMILL
GYMBO'S
BEEP!
CONGRATULATIONS
320 kcal

BEEP!
TURTLE SPEED
BEEP
BEEP
SPEED UP

BEEP!
BEEP!
BEEP!
MOUNTAIN MODE
START
BEEP!

RABID DOG
MODE
START
BEEP
BEEP
BEEP
BEEP
MURDER
MODE
START

BEEP!
STOP!
ZOOOOOOO

GYMBO'S
CONGRATULATIONS
001 kcal
END

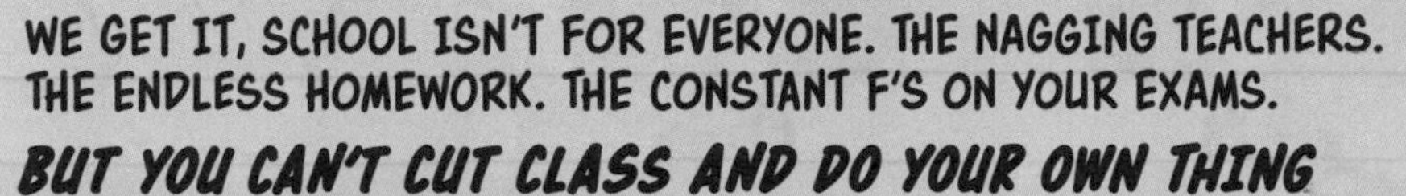
WE GET IT, SCHOOL ISN'T FOR EVERYONE. THE NAGGING TEACHERS.
THE ENDLESS HOMEWORK. THE CONSTANT F'S ON YOUR EXAMS.
BUT YOU CAN'T CUT CLASS AND DO YOUR OWN THING
WITHOUT GETTING IN TROUBLE, RIGHT?... WRONG!!

ALWAYS BE SAFE WHEN USING SCISSORS. ASK AN ADULT FOR HELP!
Get Out of School
FREE CARD™
- THIS CARD IS VALID FOR ONE FREE DAY OUT OF SCHOOL.* -
*EXPIRES: MARCH 1999
THIS COOL CARD IS ACCEPTED BY MOST MAJOR EDUCATIONAL INSTITUTIONS. ELEMENTARY SCHOOLS, HIGH SCHOOLS, WIZARD SCHOOLS, SCHOOLS OF FISH— YOU NAME IT!
JUST CONFIDENTLY PRESENT IT TO THE MOST SENIOR MEMBER OF YOUR FACULTY AND BAM—
YOU'RE OFF THE HOOK!
SCHOOL
YOU CAN CUT OUT YOUR VERY OWN GET OUT OF SCHOOL FREE CARD™ AND BECOME FLUENT IN BEING TRUANT TODAY!

Get Out of School
FREE CARD™
BE SURE TO GET HELP FROM AN ADULT!

MEANWHILE... AT AN EXTREMELY FANCY RESTAURANT...
FLY ME TO THE SOUP

SPLASH!

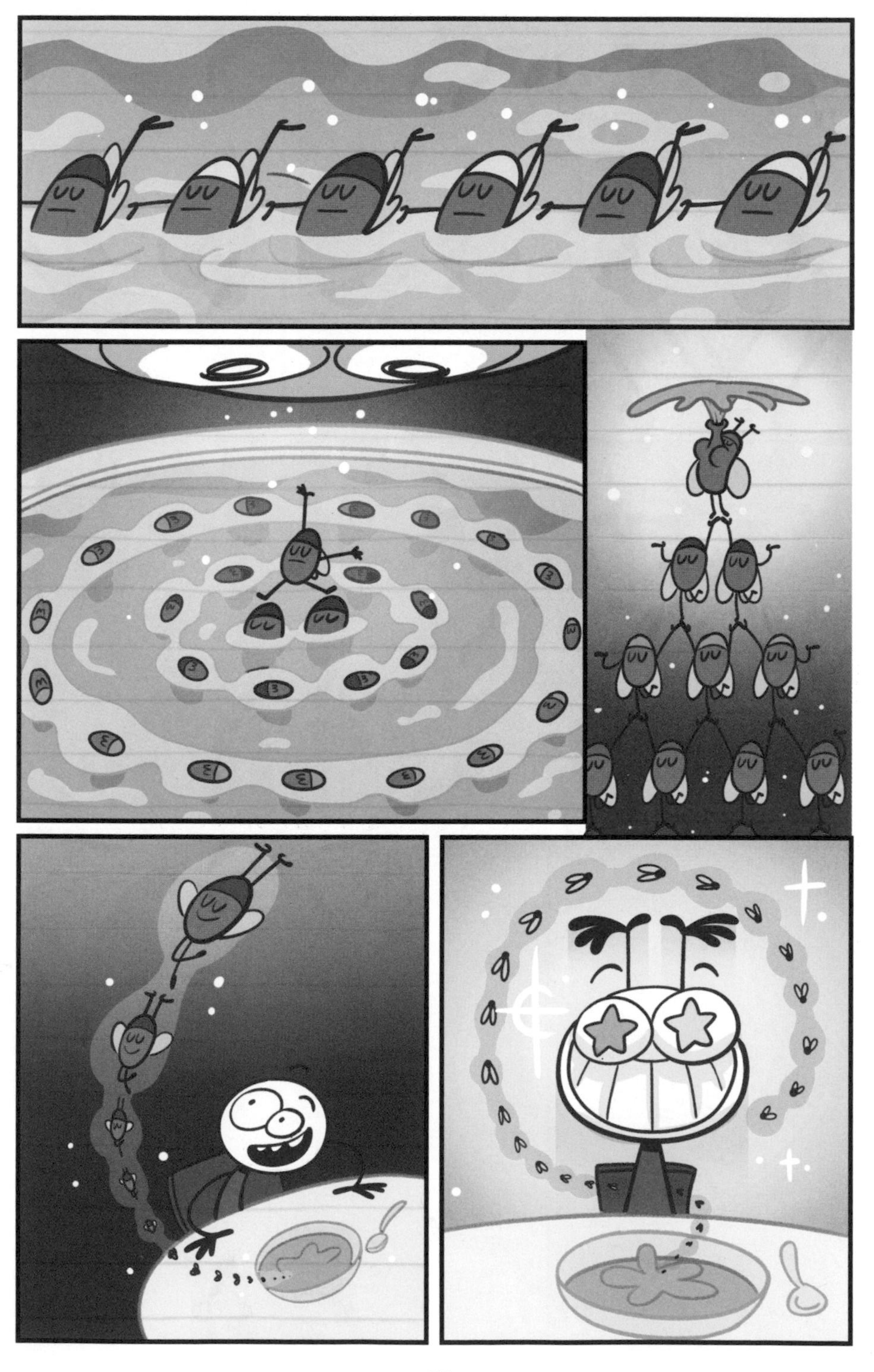

END

YET ANOTHER PEACEFUL DAY IN PENCILOPOLIS...
IF
Looks
Could
KILL
PSYCH!
CRASH
TREMBLIN' TENTACLES... IT'S OCTO-ZILLA, FRESH OUT OF AQUA-JAIL AND READY TO TERRORIZE PENCILOPOLIS ONCE AGAIN!

THIS LOOKS LIKE A JOB FOR...
ZIP!!
POW!
SUPER PENCILMISS
P

HOTDOG
SHINING WITH THE LIGHT OF JUSTICE!
SHE'S THE GREATEST SUPERHERO OF THEM ALL!
HER POWERS WILL MAKE SEAFOOD OUT OF THIS CREATURE!
ACK!!
BUT WHAT'S THIS?

A CLASSY LOAFER AND WHISPER OF GLITTER, IT'S NONE OTHER THAN PENCILMISS'S LOYAL STYLIST!
UNFORTUNATELY FOR SUPER PENCILMISS, A TEAM OF SUPER-STYLISTS NEVER STRAYS FAR FROM THEIR HERO!
DARLING, WE CAN'T HAVE YOU KICKING OCTO-BUTT LOOKING LIKE A SAD TOWEL!

BRACE YOURSELF FOR A TOTAL PENCILMISS MAKEOVER!
CLAP CLAP!
?
Gor-geous!
CUTE!
SLEEK!
PFFT!?

SUPER
FASHION
THEY SAY THAT LOOKS CAN KILL...
IT'S TIME TO PUT THAT TO THE TEST!
PENCILMISS ROCKETS FORWARD HEROICALLY!
SAY CHEESE!!
!?
UNTIL...

OH NO, THE DREADED PAPARAZZI! THEY ARE HOOKED ON PENCILMISS'S NEW LOOK!
HA! HA! HA!
IN THE DISTANCE, OCTO-ZILLA MOCKS THIS WIMPY DISPLAY OF FASHION.

NO OBSTACLE TOO GREAT, OUR HERO PUSHES PAST THE PICTURE PUSHERS TOWARD HER FIENDISH FOE!
...OR NOT!
SPLAT!!
DISASTER, YET AGAIN! A BROKEN HEEL!
IT LOOKS LIKE PENCILMISS'S LOOKS MIGHT BE KILLING HER!

PENCILMISS'S STYLIST IS FURIOUS ABOUT THIS FOOTWEAR FATALITY!
NOW HIS TEAM MUST START FROM SCRATCH!
POF
BIFF
MEANWHILE, OCTO-ZILLA KEEPS LAUGHING...
HA HA HA HA HA HA
AND LAUGHING...
HA HA HA HA
HA HA HA HA HA HA HA
AND LAUGHING AND...

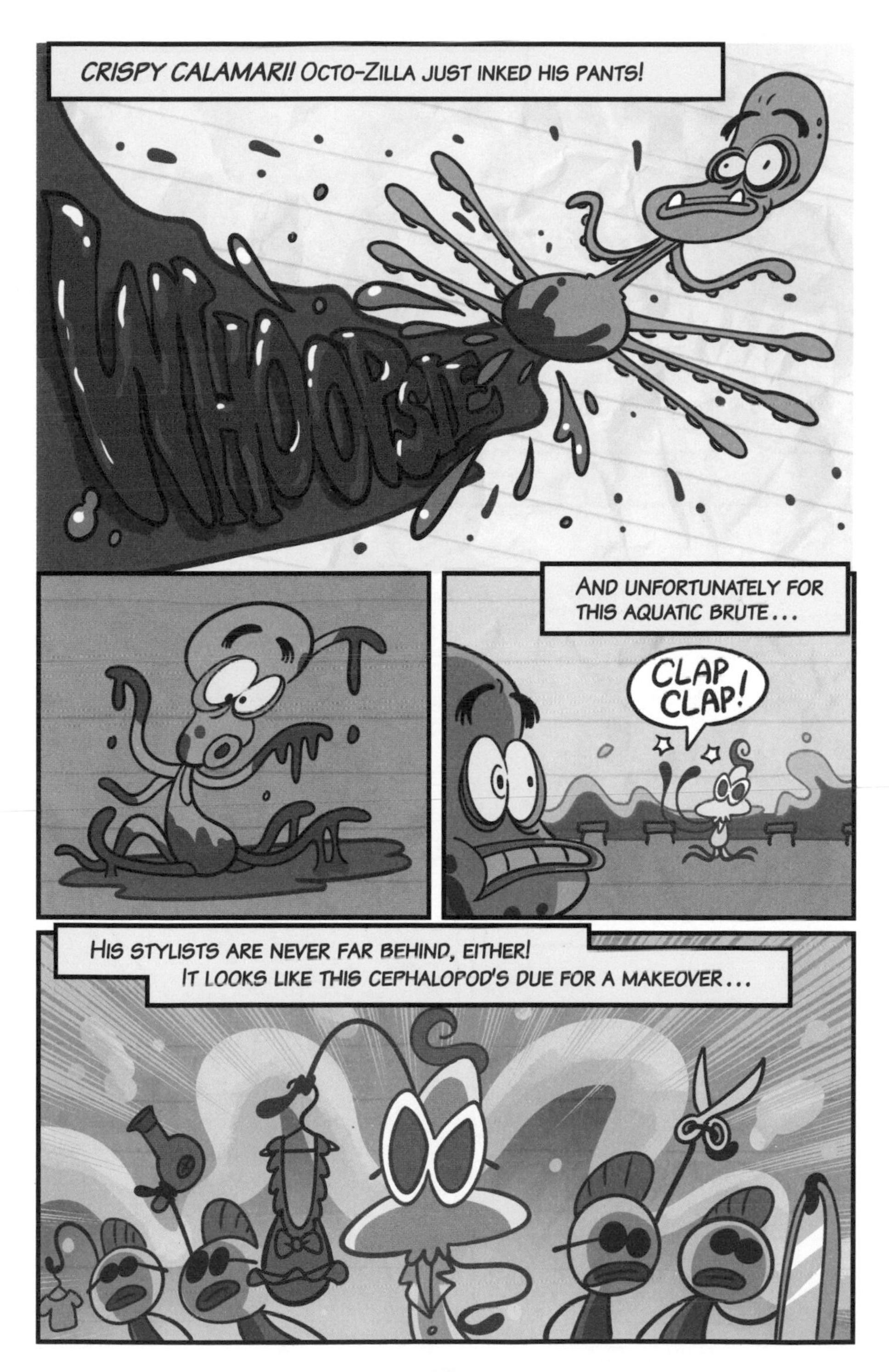
CRISPY CALAMARI! OCTO-ZILLA JUST INKED HIS PANTS!
WHOOPSIE
AND UNFORTUNATELY FOR THIS AQUATIC BRUTE...
CLAP CLAP!
HIS STYLISTS ARE NEVER FAR BEHIND, EITHER!
IT LOOKS LIKE THIS CEPHALOPOD'S DUE FOR A MAKEOVER...

STYLISTS IN HOT PURSUIT OF PENCILMISS!
STYLISTS IN HOT PURSUIT OF OCTO-ZILLA!
WILL THEY EVER ESCAPE THIS FASHIONABLE INFANTRY?

YES, THEY WILL!
PUFF
SPRAY
NICE LIPS!!
SNIP
STRIKE POSE!

HIGH ABOVE THE FRAY, SUPER PENCILMISS AND OCTO-ZILLA LEARN THE MOST CRUCIAL RULE OF BEING A HERO:
HOT!
VOUGE!
TRENDY
CURRENT!
SWAG
BURP!
BURRRPP
"AN ENEMY OF MY STYLIST IS A FRIEND OF MINE."
HA
HA
HA
END

Do you want the world to know that your BFF is yours, **ALL YOURS??**

With **BEST FRIEND HANDCUFFS**, you may not be joined at the hip, but you will be chained at the wrist!

These are genuine police-grade handcuffs. Forged with stainless steel, you can rest easy knowing your best friend will never be more than an arm's length away!

BEST FRIEND HANDCUFFS
ship with no key!

Once they're latched,
you're attached!

*Best friend not included.

FLAKE IT TILL YOU MAKE IT
EGGS
CEREAL
CARDS
DING!
!
SEVERE
WEATHER
WARNING
DING
DING
DING

SANITARY SUPPLIES
GREETING CARDS
CRITICALWEATHER
WARNING
WARNING
WARNING
WHAP

...??
DING!
CATASTROPHIC WEATHER IMMINENT
WWEEEEEEEEEEEEE
MART
CRASH!!
END

MEANWHILE, AT THE LIBRARY...
RIGHT BACK ACHOO!
A...
ACHOO!
BLESS YOU!
A...
ACHOO
...

?
ACHOO!
...
ACHOO
...
...
...
...
...
...
...
!!!

ACHOO!
...
ACHOO
OFF
...
ACHOO!
...
AAAA CHOO!
...
AACHOO!!
COOK

ACHOO
ACHOO
ACHOO
ACHOO
ACHOO
ACHOO
ACHOO!!!...
SHHH...
SILENCE
ACHOO! ACHOO!!
ACHOO-CHOO
CHOO!!!...
!?

Library
!#?!

Bless You!
Bless You!
END

ALMOIST FAMOUS
WE FIND OURSELVES ON AN ARID DESERT PLANET... NO LIFE CAN POSSIBLY EXIST IN THIS BRUTAL, UNFORGIVING ATMOSPHERE!
OH... ACTUALLY, IT'S JUST PENCILMATE'S GROSS DRY HANDS.
Bleh!
THIS CALLS FOR SOME LUBULAR ACTION!
IT'S MOISTURIZIN' TIME!!!
HE SCOURS THE BATHROOM CABINET UNTIL HE SPOTS THE GOODS.

SNAG!
LOOKS LIKE THEY STOPPED MAKING THIS STUFF AGES AGO!
Granny's
HOMEMADE
Skin
moisturizer
EXTRA STRENGTH
USE BY: 1990
EH, WHAT COULD POSSIBLY GO WRONG?
SPLORT

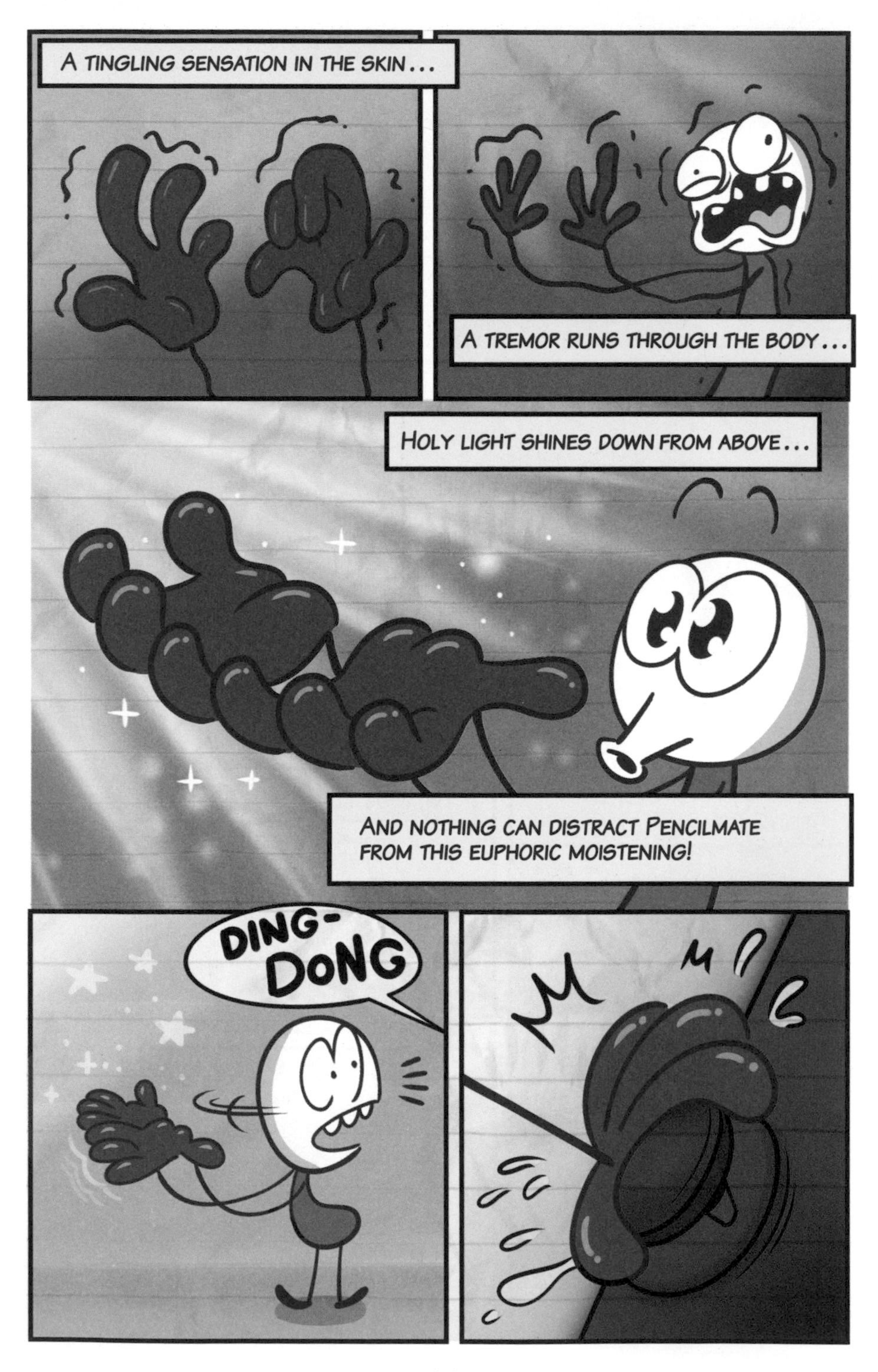
A TINGLING SENSATION IN THE SKIN...
A TREMOR RUNS THROUGH THE BODY...
HOLY LIGHT SHINES DOWN FROM ABOVE...
AND NOTHING CAN DISTRACT PENCILMATE FROM THIS EUPHORIC MOISTENING!
DING-DONG

AT HIS FRONT DOOR, PENCILMATE FINDS A HUMBLE DELIVERYMAN...
...WHOSE LIFE IS ABOUT TO CHANGE FOREVER.

UH, NICE GUY!
MAYBE TOO NICE.
PENCILMATE BIDS THE MAN GOOD DAY, MAKING A MENTAL NOTE TO REQUEST A DIFFERENT DELIVERY PERSON NEXT TIME.
SLAM
BUT LITTLE DID PENCILMATE REALIZE THAT ONCE PROPERLY GREASED, NEWS TRAVELS FAST...

THE DELIVERYMAN CALLS EVERYONE HE KNOWS...
?
HANDS.
HANDS?
HANDS!
HANDS!
AND EVERYONE HE KNOWS CALLS EVERYONE THEY KNOW...
HAVE YOU HEARD ABOUT THE HANDS?
AND IT ISN'T LONG BEFORE THOSE HANDS ARE THE HOTTEST TALK IN THE LAND!
HANDS

BACK IN HIS LIVING ROOM, PENCILMATE RELAXES WITH A GOOD BOOK.
The Fart Academy
Fartis Gratia Fartis
BUT HIS RELAXATION IS SUDDENLY INTERRUPTED...
SLAM!!
BY A MEDIA CIRCUS! THE PRESS HAS GOTTEN WIND OF PENCILMATE'S IMPOSSIBLY SMOOTH HANDS!
DISPLAY THOSE BEAUTIFUL MITTS, KID! YOU'RE ABOUT TO BE A FOUR-FINGERED STAR!

AND A STAR HE IS. HIS HANDS WIN HIM LEGIONS OF FANS.
HOT HANDS
THE MOST PERFECT HANDS
EVERYBODY WANTS TO WORSHIP AT THE ALTAR OF THEIR SMOOTHNESS.
SPLORT
LIFE IS DIFFERENT FOR PENCILMATE AFTER THAT FIRST, FATEFUL SQUIRT.
HANDS!
HANDS!
HANDS
HANDS!

WAVE
WAVE
EEEEK!!
HANDS
HANDS
HANDS
HE IS BIGGER THAN THE BEATLES, ELVIS, AND RIGHT SAID FRED, ALL ROLLED INTO ONE!
HANDS
HANDS
HANDS
HANDS
HAND POWER
HANDS
LIVE
HANDS
SHOW US THE HANDS
LEFT 6% RIGHT
HIS HAND IS THE SLICIEST THING SINCE HOT BREAD!

EVERYWHERE HE GOES, PEOPLE WANT A PIECE OF HIM!
...A VERY SPECIFIC PIECE OF HIM, TO BE EXACT.
BUT IT APPEARS THAT PENCILMATE'S HAND HAS ATTRACTED A SUPERFAN!
WHO COULD THIS MYSTERIOUS FIGURE BE??

IT'S THE DELIVERYMAN FROM EARLIER!
THE MAN OBSESSED WITH A HAND
AND HE'S STOCKPILED PICTURES OF PENCILMATE'S HAND!
CLEARLY HE'S INFATUATED!
BACK AT PENCILMATE'S ABODE, WE FIND OUR NEW CELEBRITY RESPONDING TO FAN MAIL.
SLAM!
BUT HE'S INTERRUPTED ONCE AGAIN! AND THIS TIME, IT'S HIS DERANGED #1 FAN!

THIS GUY HAS TRULY FALLEN HAND OVER HEELS! HE WANTS TO HOLD PENCILMATE'S PERFECTLY PLUSH PAW...
FOREVER!!!
BEST
FRIENDS
AHHHHHHHHHH

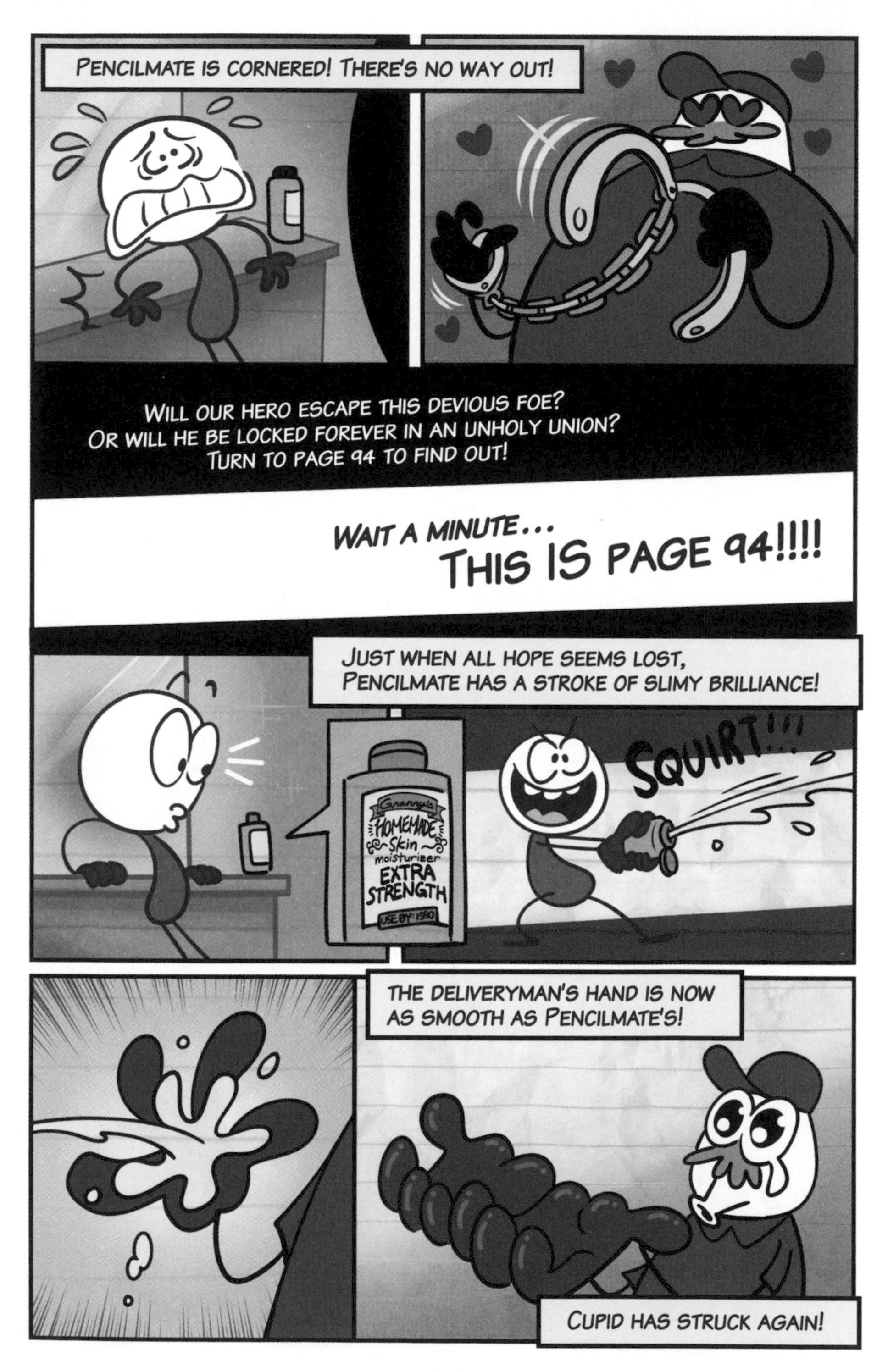
PENCILMATE IS CORNERED! THERE'S NO WAY OUT!
WILL OUR HERO ESCAPE THIS DEVIOUS FOE?
OR WILL HE BE LOCKED FOREVER IN AN UNHOLY UNION?
TURN TO PAGE 94 TO FIND OUT!
WAIT A MINUTE...
THIS IS PAGE 94!!!!
JUST WHEN ALL HOPE SEEMS LOST,
PENCILMATE HAS A STROKE OF SLIMY BRILLIANCE!
Granny's
HOMEMADE
Skin
moisturizer
EXTRA
STRENGTH
USE BY: 1990
SQUIRT!!!
THE DELIVERYMAN'S HAND IS NOW
AS SMOOTH AS PENCILMATE'S!
CUPID HAS STRUCK AGAIN!

HE SLAPS THE HANDCUFFS ONTO HIMSELF AND SKIPS OFF INTO THE SUNSET WITH LOVE.
LOCK!
WHEW! THAT WAS A CLOSE CALL!
ALL THIS EXCITEMENT HAS DRIED OUT HIS EPIDERMIS! TIME FOR SOME MORE OF THAT TRUSTY HAND CREAM!
WHEW
FLORT!
...
HE'S ALL OUT! AND THIS WAS THE VERY LAST BOTTLE EVER MADE!!!
NOOOOOOO!
I MARRIED MY HAND
PENCILMATE BREAKS DOWN!
OH WELL, IT WAS NICE WHILE IT LASTED!
END

Knock on PENCILWOOD
MEANWHILE, IN PENCILWOOD...
PENCILWOOD
ROSS BOLLINGER
!?
PENCILMISS

PENCIL
PENCILMATE
PENCIL
...

BRR-R-R-R-R-R
PENCILMATE

PENCILMISS
—THE—
MOVIE
MINI-PENCILM
CEREAL
Granny
MEET
BIG GUY
Pencil-
Miss
STAR
HOTTEST
OF THE
MONTH
MISS
TALL
NOW
BIG
PENCILMATE
PENCILWOOD
MINI
Pencilmiss
TALL
GUY
END

Pump My Ride
$
$
PRICE
$ 19.89
GALLONS
HERE STANDS PENCILMATE, 11 CENTS AWAY FROM $20.
...
ROLL..
19.99
EASY DOES IT...
!
THERE!
PING!
20.01
WHOOPS... ONE CENT OVER!
BETTER LUCK NEXT TIME!

.01
.01
.01
.01
.01
.01
.01
.01
.01
.01
.01
.01
WHOA, LOOKS LIKE HE'S GOING FOR $30!
SQUEEZE
PING!
30.02
WHOOPS AGAIN!
PING!
40.01
...AND AGAIN!

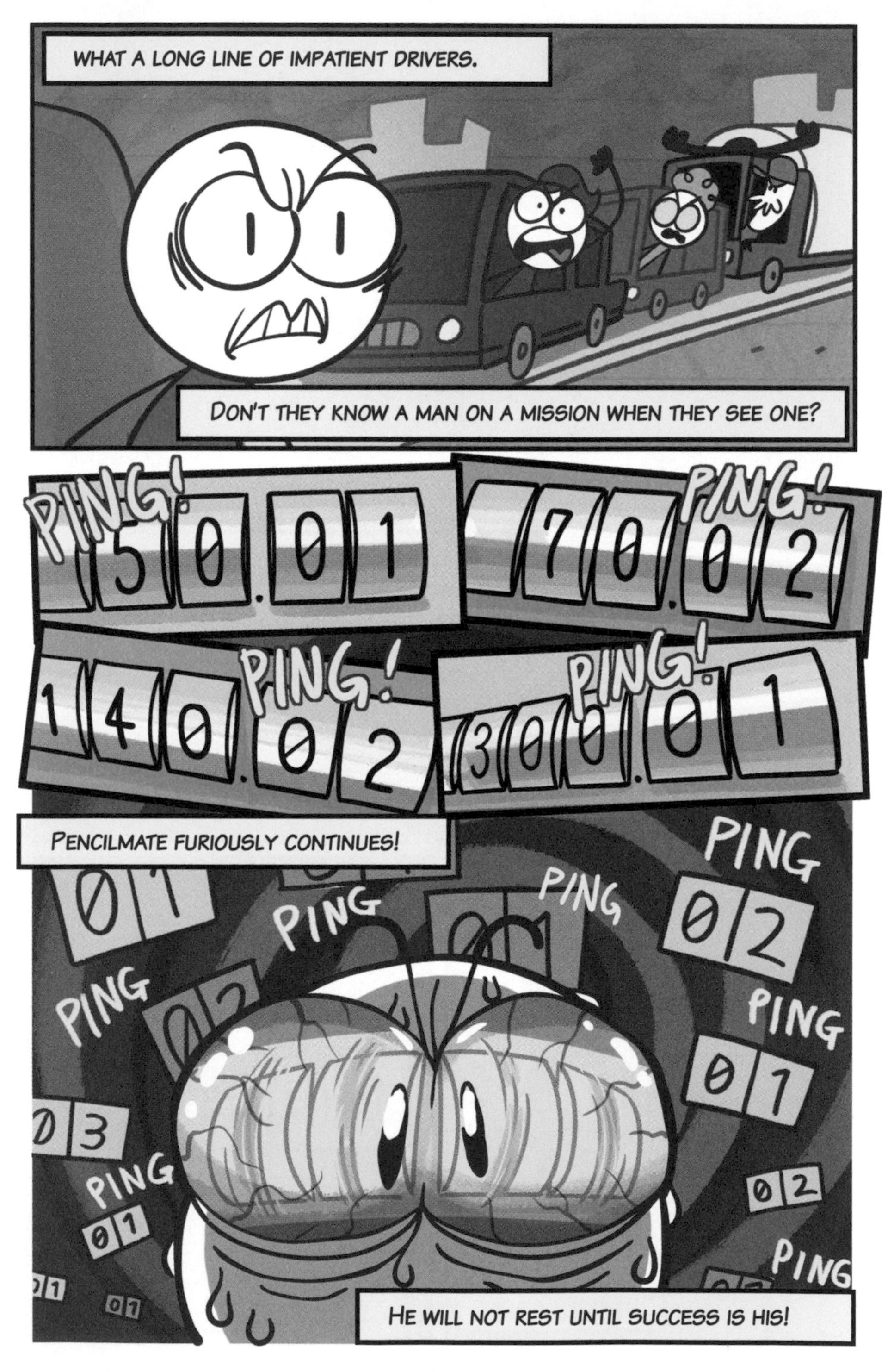
WHAT A LONG LINE OF IMPATIENT DRIVERS.
DON'T THEY KNOW A MAN ON A MISSION WHEN THEY SEE ONE?
PING!
50.01
PING!
70.02
PING!
140.02
PING!
300.01
PENCILMATE FURIOUSLY CONTINUES!
PING
PING
PING
PING
PING
PING
PING
HE WILL NOT REST UNTIL SUCCESS IS HIS!

PING!
$1000.00
FINALLY, A ROUND NUMBER!
SUCCESS WAS EXPENSIVE, BUT HE'S DONE IT!
AND YOU CAN NEVER PUT A PRICE ON VICTORY!
GUSH
...EVEN IF YOU MAKE A TOTAL GAS OF YOURSELF.
END

ALL THUMBS

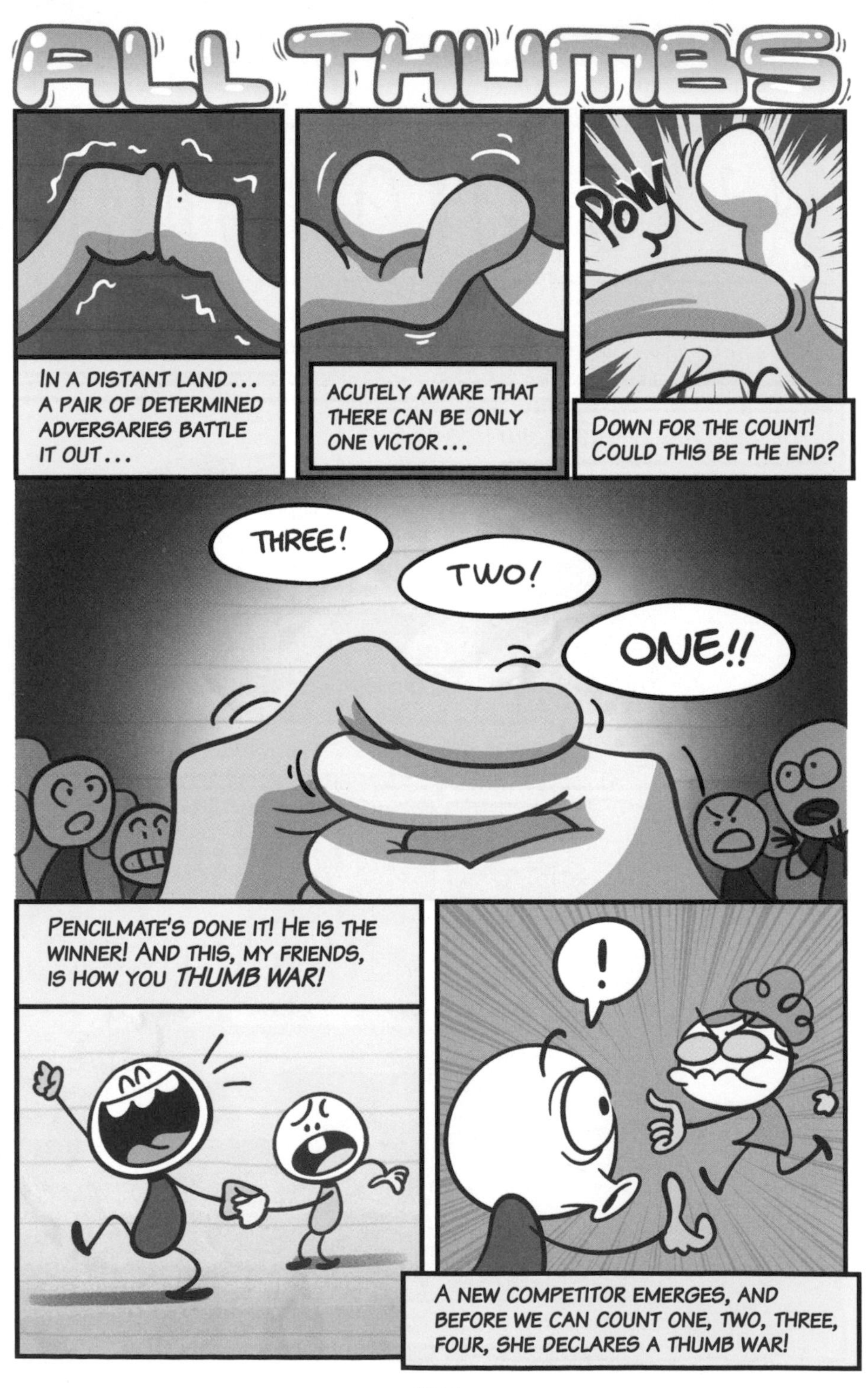

In a distant land... a pair of determined adversaries battle it out...
Acutely aware that there can be only one victor...
POW
Down for the count! Could this be the end?
THREE!
TWO!
ONE!!
Pencilmate's done it! He is the winner! And this, my friends, is how you *THUMB WAR!*
!
A new competitor emerges, and before we can count one, two, three, four, she declares a thumb war!

AND THE FASTER THEY COME, THE HARDER THEY FALL!
PENCILMATE IS TOTALLY AWE-THUMB!!
THUMB & THUMBER
UNDERDOG STRIKES AGAIN!!
CRITICS GIVE TWO BRUISED THUMBS-UP!
BUT WHAT STANDS BETWEEN PENCILMATE AND THE ULTIMATE TRIUMPH?
TONIGHT ONLY!
PENCILMATE
VS
THUMB WAR CHAMP
UH-OH, IT'S THIS GUY!
THUMB WAR CHAMPION

IN THIS CORNER, THE THUMB WAR CHAMPION OF THE WORLD...
OL' IRON THUMB!
IT'S THE PEAK OF EVOLUTION, FOLKS! ALL THAT THUMB DOES IS EAT, SLEEP, AND TEXT!
AAAAND IN THIS CORNER...
PENCILMATE.
DROOP

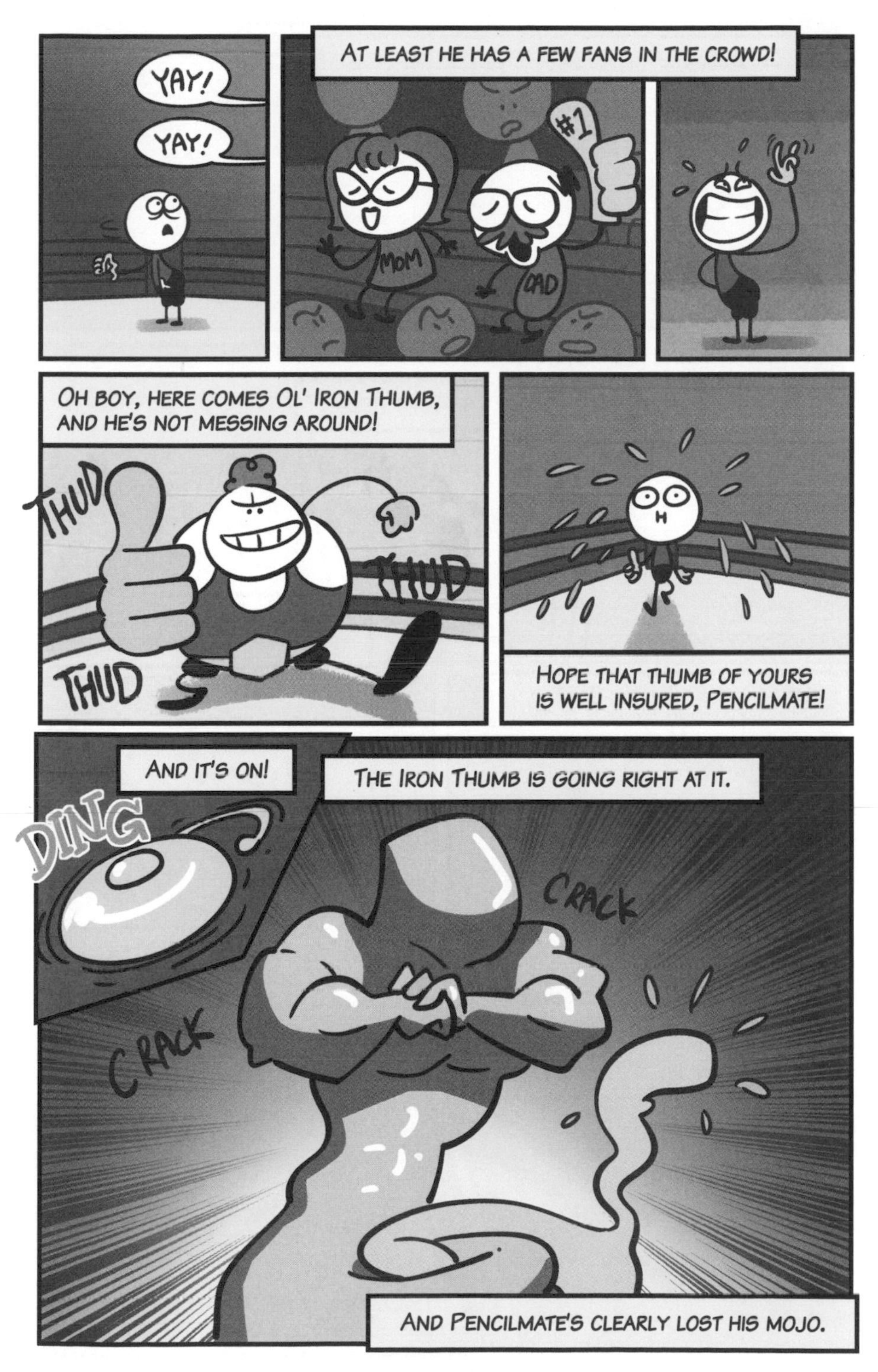
YAY!
YAY!
AT LEAST HE HAS A FEW FANS IN THE CROWD!
#1
MOM
DAD
OH BOY, HERE COMES OL' IRON THUMB, AND HE'S NOT MESSING AROUND!
THUD
THUD
THUD
HOPE THAT THUMB OF YOURS IS WELL INSURED, PENCILMATE!
AND IT'S ON!
THE IRON THUMB IS GOING RIGHT AT IT.
DING
CRACK
CRACK
AND PENCILMATE'S CLEARLY LOST HIS MOJO.

THIS IS GOING TO BE AN EASY ONE FOR THE CHAMP.
BUT WHAT'S THIS?! LEFT HOOK!
RIGHT HOOK!
PENCILMATE'S THUMB KEEPS WIGGLING OUT OF THE WAY!
EVEN THE CHAMP HAS NEVER SEEN ANYTHING LIKE IT!
FOLKS, THIS IS STILL ANYONE'S MATCH! THE SPORT MAY NEVER BE THE SAME AGAIN!
IRON THUMB IS REALLY FLAGGING. HE'S FEELING THE PRESSURE!
UNBELIEVABLE! THE IRON THUMB HAS USED UP ALL OF HIS ENERGY!

PENCILMATE'S NOODLE THUMB HAS MOVED IN FOR THE PIN!
THREE!
TWO!!
ONE!!
I CAN'T BELIEVE MY EYES! WE ARE WITNESSING HISTORY IN THE MAKING!

LADIES AND GENTLEMEN, THE NEW THUMB CHAMPION OF THE WORLD...
#1
PENCILMATE!
#1
NEW CHAMP
YAY!
WOOHOO!!
WOOT!
LATER THAT EVENING, PENCILMATE CELEBRATES HIS VICTORY WITH HIS TWO BIGGEST FANS.
MOM
DAD
UH-OH! IT LOOKS LIKE OL' IRON THUMB HAS INTERRUPTED THIS TENDER MOMENT!

COULD HE BE SEEKING RETRIBUTION?
OKAY!
OH! WHAT AN UNEXPECTED GESTURE OF GOOD SPORTSMANSHIP FROM THE FORMER CHAMP!
AND A FITTING RESPONSE FROM PENCILMATE!
OKAY...!
JUST REMEMBER, KIDS, SORE LOSERS STICK OUT LIKE SORE THUMBS.
SCREECH!
SO HERE'S A THUMBS-UP TO ALL THE GOOD SPORTS OUT THERE.
AND UNTIL NEXT TIME...
ZOOOOM!
THUMB'S THE WORD!
END

PUT THE PEBBLE TO THE METAL
ANOTHER PERFECT DAY FOR PENCILMATE!
ANOTHER PERFECT DAY FOR PENCILMATE!
ANOTHER PERFECT DAY FOR...

YEEEOOOCHHH!!!
ANOTHER PERFECT DAY FOR ROCK MONSTER!
OHH!
OUCH!
EEK!
END

TURN THE PAGE FOR...
PAPER CLOTHING FOR PENCILS!
BE SURE TO GET HELP FROM AN ADULT!

STUCK WITH A **DISTRESSINGLY DRAB** PENCIL? BRIGHTEN UP YOUR WRITIN' WITH CLOTHES FOR YOUR FAVORITE UTENSIL! DRESS YOUR **NO. 2** IN ONE OF THESE JAW-DROPPING OUTFITS TO MAKE IT LOOK AS **FANCY** AS YOU FEEL!

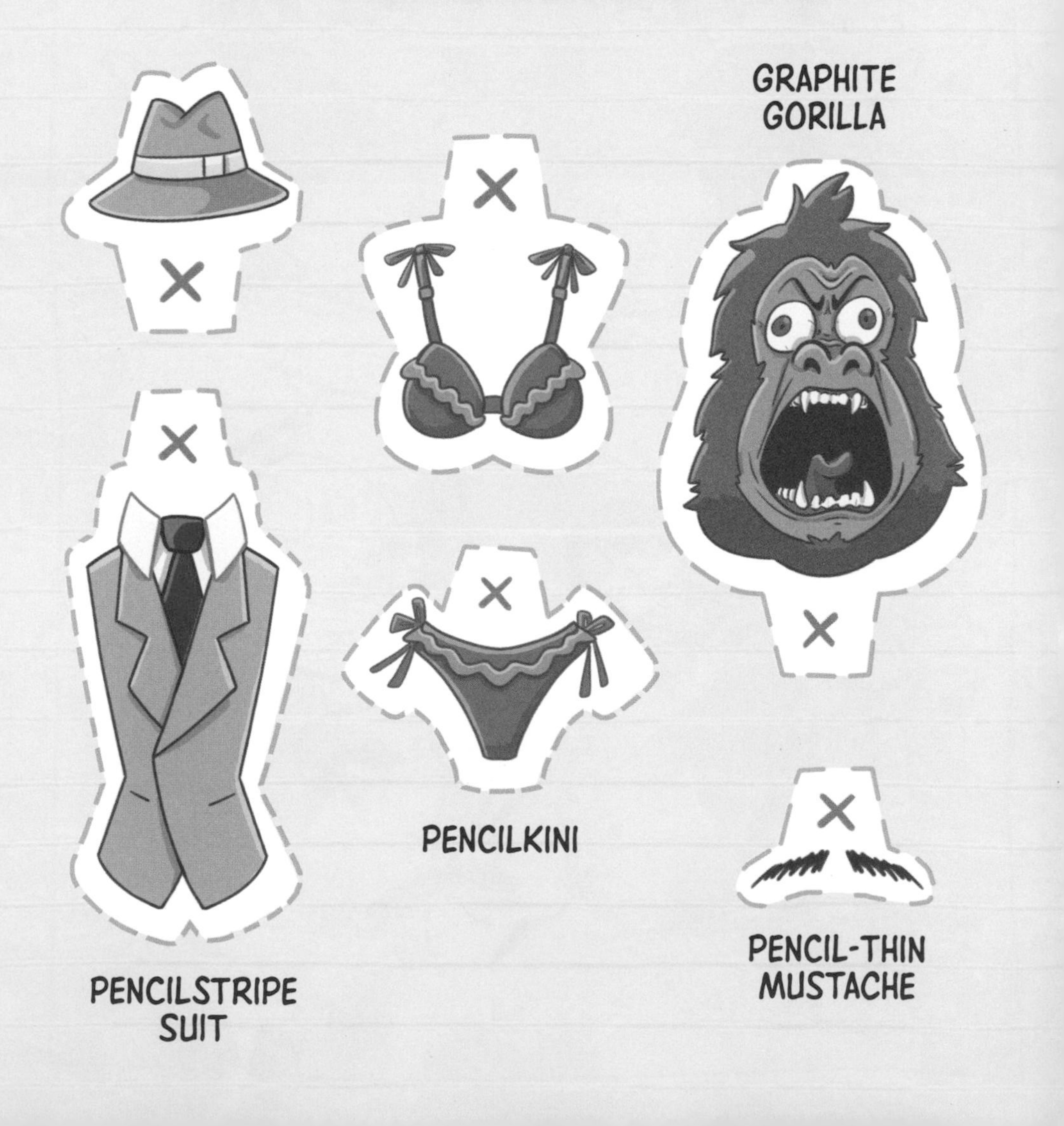

CLIP OUT THE CLOTHES, POKE YOUR PENCIL THROUGH THE TAB, AND GET THAT STATIONERY CATWALK READY!

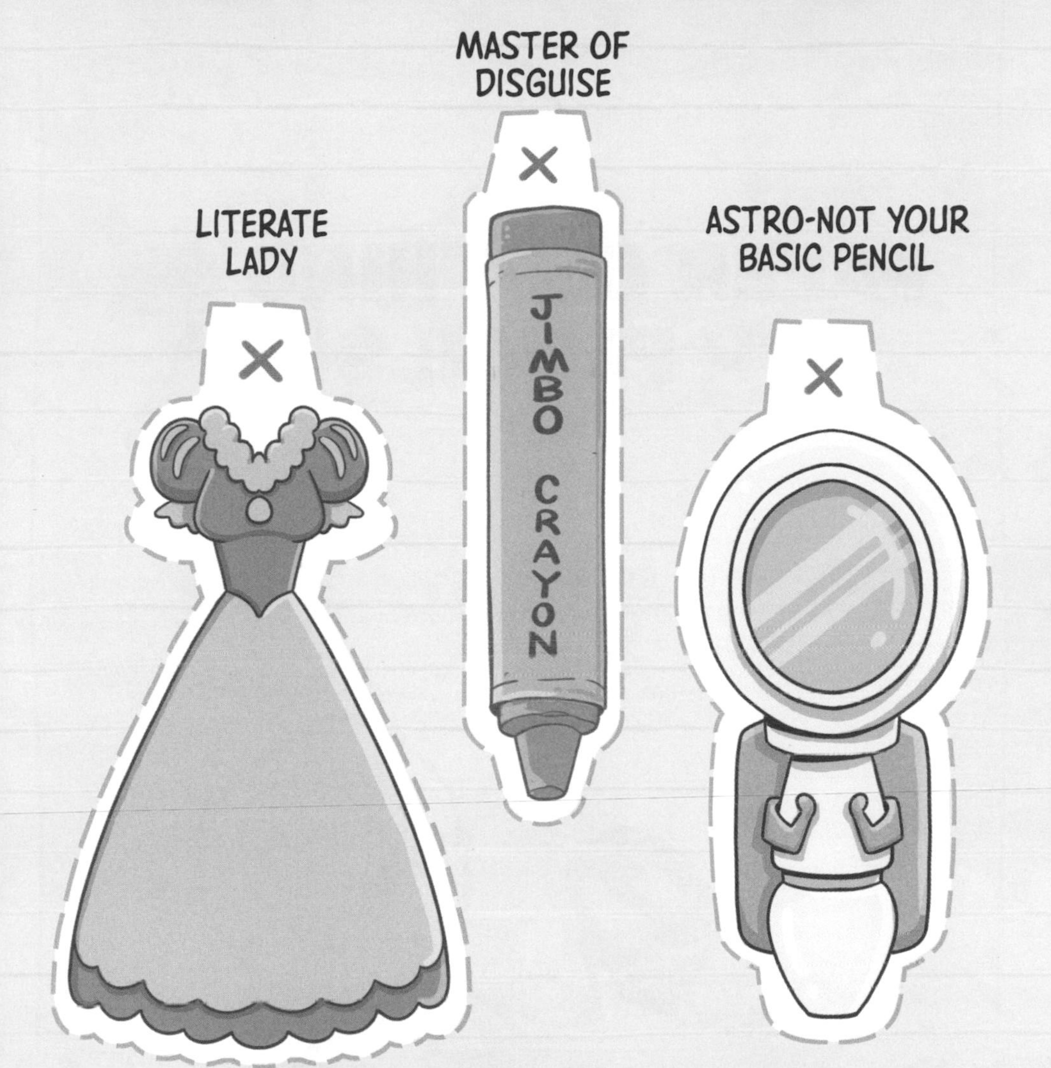

NOW AT THE INCREDIBLY LOW PRICE OF **ABSOLUTELY FREE**, PAPER CLOTHING FOR PENCILS ARE FLYING OFF THE PAGE!

CUT OUT YOURS AND COVER YOUR NAKED PENCIL TODAY!

...OR TOMORROW, OR WHENEVER!

ALWAYS BE SAFE WHEN USING SCISSORS. ASK AN ADULT FOR HELP!

PAPER CLOTHING
FOR PENCILS!
P
BE SURE TO
GET HELP
FROM AN
ADULT!

BIPPITY BOPPITY BUMMER
ONCE UPON A TIME, THERE WAS A BEAUTIFUL, KIND YOUNG DOODLE NAMED PENCILMISS.
EVERY DAY, HER STEPSISTERS WOULD BEHAVE LIKE TOTAL PIGS.
AND EVERY DAY, PENCILMISS WOULD PATIENTLY CLEAN UP THEIR MESS.
@#$
BUT ONE DAY, FATE CAME KNOCKING AT HER DOOR, QUITE LITERALLY.
KNOCK! KNOCK!
A ROYAL MESSENGER ARRIVED WITH A MOST FORTUITOUS ANNOUNCEMENT:

THE PRINCE WAS THROWING A BALL, AND ALL ELIGIBLE BACHELORETTES WERE INVITED!
YOU'RE INVITED
THE STEPSISTERS WERE BESIDE THEMSELVES.
YOU'RE INVITED
A PRINCE, SINGLE AND READY TO JINGLE HIS FORTUNE INTO HIS FUTURE WIFE'S PURSE? A DREAM COME TRUE!
THEY HURRIEDLY DEPARTED, LEAVING POOR PENCILMISS HOME ALONE WITH SOUR GRAPES.
IF ONLY THERE WERE SOMEONE TO RESCUE HER FROM ANOTHER NIGHT OF GRUELING CHORES.
A PIXIE AUNT? A SPIRIT SIBLING? OR EVEN A NYMPH NANNY?

WELL, WHADDYA KNOW...
...A FAIRY GODMOTHER!
ZAP
POOT!
OKAY, MAYBE A DISCOUNT FAIRY GODMOTHER...
BUT THAT'S BETTER THAN NOTHING!
WITH A SWISH OF THE MAGIC WAND, PENCILMISS'S TATTERED CLOTHES TRANSFORMED INTO A BEAUTIFUL—
POOF!
MY WORD, THE 1600S CALLED AND THEY WANT THEIR DRESS BACK!
HER WORK FINISHED, FAIRY GODMOTHER WAS ITCHING TO GET GOING AND PLAY SLOTS AT YE OLDE CASINO.
BUT PENCILMISS WASN'T READY TO GIVE UP HER DREAMS JUST YET!
VAGUE
HOT
SO SHE POLITELY REQUESTED A DRESS MORE SUITED TO MODERN TASTE.

WITH A QUICK THOUGHT AND ANOTHER SWISH, FAIRY GODMOTHER ATTEMPTED TO HONOR PENCILMISS'S REQUEST AGAIN.
AND AGAIN.
AND AGAIN.
AND... AGAIN.
UNTIL FAIRY GODMOTHER FINALLY LANDED ON THE PERFECT LOOK.
OR... NOT.

SUDDENLY THE CASTLE BELLS TOLLED. THE BALL HAD BEGUN, AND PENCILMISS WAS OUT OF TIME!
DONG!
DONG!
DONG!
DRESS OR NOT, OUR BRAVE HEROINE DECIDED NOTHING WOULD KEEP HER FROM THIS FANCY DANCE.
POOF
BUT FAIRY GODMOTHER WASN'T GIVING UP THAT EASILY.
LOOK! SPARKLING GLASS SLIPPERS!
CRASH
CRASH
UNFORTUNATELY, MAKING SHOES OUT OF GLASS WAS A DUMB IDEA.
WITH GREAT FURY, PENCILMISS MARCHED DOWN THE STREET AS FAST AS HER INJURED FEET WOULD CARRY HER.

BUT FAIRY G WAS DESPERATE TO MAKE AMENDS BY GIFTING PENCILMISS A PUMPKIN CARRIAGE!
ZAP!
SPLAT!
OR PERHAPS EVERYTHING WOULD BE FIXED WITH A DAZZLING STALLION!
POOF
MAYBE JUST TWO NORMAL COACHMEN? THAT SHOULD BE EASY.
PECK
PECK
PECK
BUT IT WAS NOT EASY!
AND NOW SHE'S REALLY LATE! PENCILMISS BETTER HURRY!

MEANWHILE, AT THE BALL, PENCILMISS'S STEPSISTERS WERE IN HOT PURSUIT OF THE PRINCE'S HEART.
WHEN—AHA!—PENCILMISS ARRIVED, SHE LOOKED . . . WELL TO BE POLITE, ABYSMAL.
THE PRINCE TURNED AND FELT HIS HEART SING THE SOULMATE SONG!
IN SPITE OF ALL HER IMPERFECTIONS, THE PRINCE KNEW SHE WAS THE ONE.
HIS TRUE LOVE WAS HERE . . .

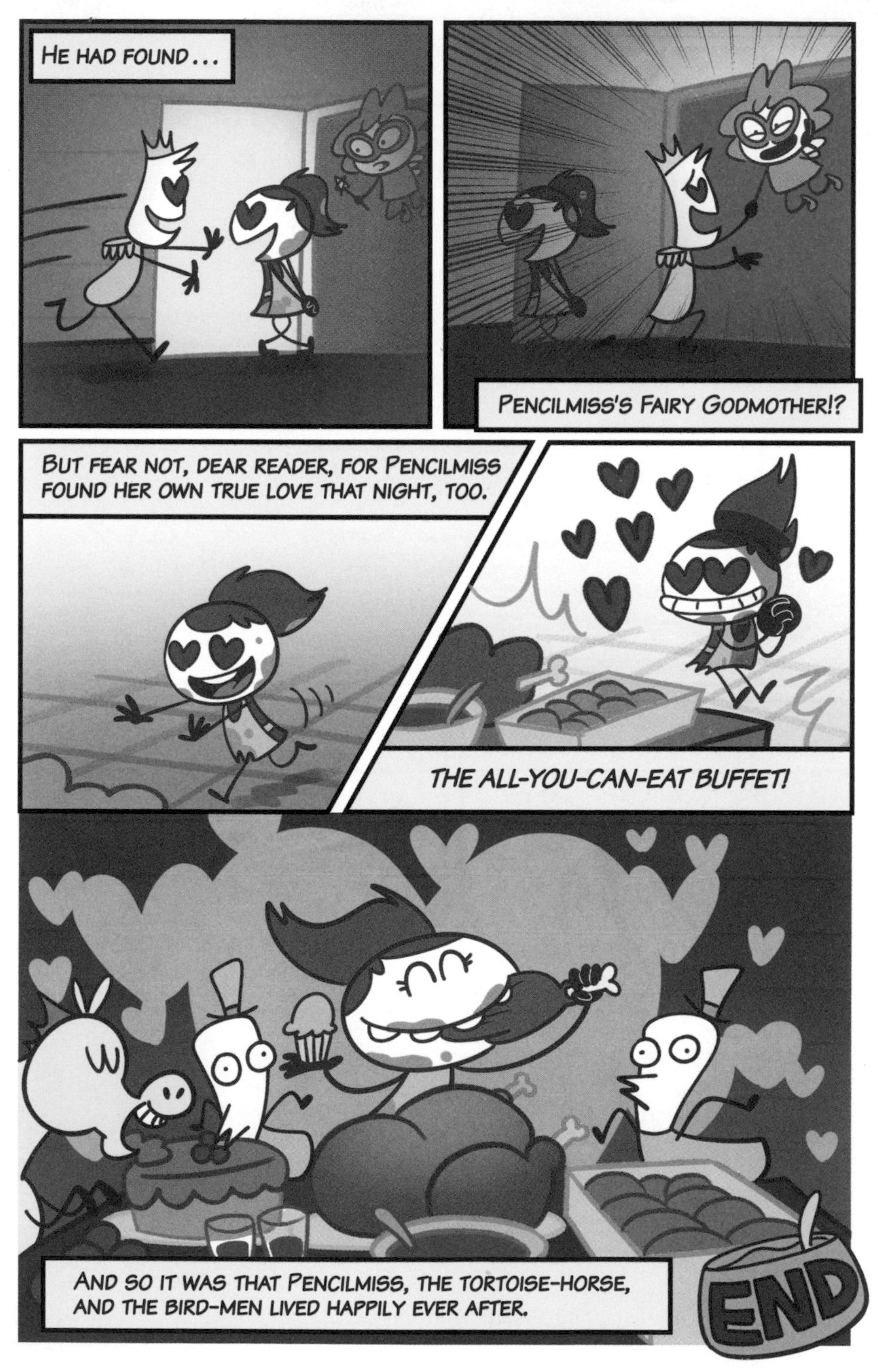
He had found...
Pencilmiss's Fairy Godmother!?
But fear not, dear reader, for Pencilmiss found her own true love that night, too.
The all-you-can-eat buffet!
And so it was that Pencilmiss, the tortoise-horse, and the bird-men lived happily ever after.
END

From the company that brought you such products as **SAD CLOWN REPELLENT, SPRAY-ON PERSONALITY,** and **THE BIONIC BUTT CHEEK** comes something brand-new . . .

GROW-A-LIMB
JUST SPRINKLE IT ON AND GROW A NEW LIMB!
Now in Strawberry Flavor!

The topical treatment that you can sprinkle just about anywhere on your body! Rub it in, and you'll sprout a new limb quicker than your friends can scream, **"HOW DID THAT GET THERE?!"**

Gain the UPPER HAND in . . .

Sports!

Self-Defense!

Pianos!

Use coupon code **11TOES** at checkout, and we'll even throw in a bottle of **Limb-B-Gone**.

! WARNING !
Keep out of reach of children

TO BEAN OR NOT TO BEAN?
JIMBO'S
BAKED BEANS
THUNK!

CRANK
CRANK
CRANK
CRANK
CRUNCH
ZIP

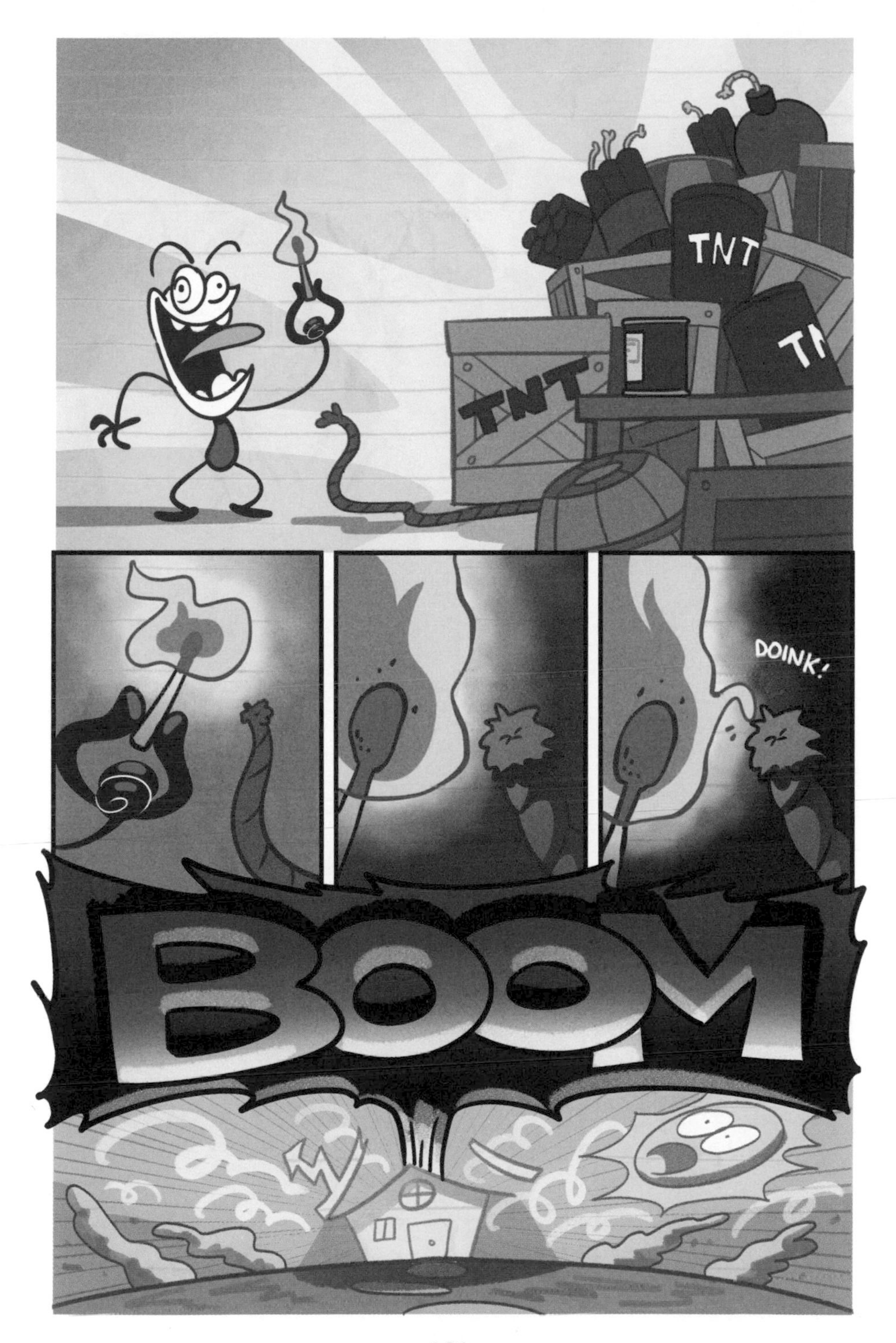
TNT
TNT
DOINK!
BOOM

JiMBO's
BAKED
THIS SIDE UP
OPEN

HA HA HA HA HA
POP
TWITCH
GULP!
AHH...
FART!
HEH HEH
END

Star TANGLED Banner
!?

END

WHEN THERE'S A JOB TO DO, PENCILMATE PUTS THE "GO" IN "GO-GETTER"!
SCORE LOSER
EGGS
MILK
BREAD
SUPERGLUE
PEANUTS
NOTHING CAN GET IN PENCILMATE'S WAY WHEN HE PUTS HIS MIND TO IT!
THE MAN IS ON A MISSION...
FLIP
FLIP
...AND FAILURE IS NOT AN OPTION!
DING!

SPEAKING OF FAILURE...
YOUR HIGH SCORE WAS BEATEN!
HIGH SCORE
1 WITCHDOC1984 701,235,845
2 PENCILM8 654,472,910
OH C'MON, PENCILMATE...
NO NEED TO GET STRESSED!
POP
POP
POP
JIMBO
JIMBO MART
SUPER SPOOKY FOREST
OKAY, FINE. ONE QUICK GAME ON THE WAY TO THE SUPERMARKET...
WAIT! WAIT! NO! TURN BACK, PENCILMATE, YOU'RE GOING THE WRONG WAY!

...IT'S NO USE! HE'S SO ENGROSSED IN HIS GAME THAT HE CAN'T HEAR US.
TRIP!
WATCH OUT!
NOOOOOOOO!
BONK!
IS THIS THE END OF PENCILMATE?
WHOSE LIFE WILL I ETERNALLY NARRATE??

ACTUALLY, HE SEEMS OKAY.
LOOKS LIKE PENCILMATE FINALLY REALIZES WHAT'S GOING ON.
I BET YOU REGRET IGNORING YOUR OLD NARRATOR PAL NOW, DON'T YOU?
ALL OF THIS COULD'VE BEEN EASILY AVOIDED IF WE DID THINGS MY WAY,
BUT NOOOOO.
POP!
POP!
YOU'RE KIDDING ME, RIGHT?

CLEARLY THINGS COULD NOT GET ANY WORSE.
EXCEPT FOR A SPOOKY HUT.
THAT'S DEFINITELY WORSE.
DO NOT ENTER, PENCILMATE!
FINE, GO RIGHT IN, I DON'T CARE.
HMM... IT APPEARS THAT SOMEONE DOESN'T LIKE PENCILMATE VERY MUCH!*
PENCILM8
SUCKS
*THAT MAKES TWO OF US

THIS CAN ONLY BE THE HOME OF...
PENCILM8 EATS POOP
PENCILMATE'S TIME KILLER 3000 ARCHNEMESIS,
WITCHDOC1984!!!
VS
SIGH I GUESS THE FINAL BATTLE FOR THE HIGH SCORE IS ON.

LET THE TAPPING COMMENCE!
TAP TAP TAP TAP TAP TAP TAP TAP TAP TAP TAP
POP POP POP POP
THIS IS NECK AND NECK!
BEEP! BEEP! BEEP! BEEP! BEEP! BEEP!

But it looks like Witchdoc1984 is out of battery!
Time for Pencilmate's big move!
BOOP!
!!!FEVER!!!
NEW HIGH SCORE!
PENCILM8
999,999,999
Well, what do you know? Pencilmate won after all!

I'M ACTUALLY QUITE PROUD OF YOU, BUDDY.
THERE'S ONLY ONE PROBLEM.
YOU FORGOT THE SHOPPING!
EGGS
MILK
BREAD
SUPERGLUE
PEANUTS
...
BUT WHEN THERE'S A JOB TO DO,
PENCILMATE PUTS THE "GO" IN "GO-GETTER"!
Ding
OH NO, NOT AGAIN!
JIMBO MART
SUPER SPOOKY FOREST
PENCILMAAAATE!!
END

SQUIRT LOCKER
SPLASH!!
SPLASH
ZONE

JIMBO'S FISH WORLD
EEE!
EEE!
SPLASH ZONE
AHHH...

SLOSH!
EEE-EEE!
SUPER
SPLASH ZONE

TOP FLOOR
SPlooSH!

SODA
SODA
EEE!
EEE!
EEE!
EEE!
SODA
EEE-EEE!
EEE-EEE!
END

ADVANCED PENCIL GRIPS

WITH GREAT PENCILS COMES GREAT RESPONSIBILITY

THESE GRIPS ARE FOR EDUCATIONAL PURPOSES ONLY.
DO NOT TRY THESE AT HOME WITHOUT EXPERT SUPERVISION!

REMEMBER:

YOU DO NOT CHOOSE THE PENCIL GRIP.
THE PENCIL GRIP CHOOSES YOU!

PROCEED WITH ABSOLUTE CAUTION.

AHH, THERE'S NOTHING LIKE HOLIDAYING AT A PICTURESQUE RURAL RETREAT...
HOST BUSTERS
JIMBO'S BNB RENTAL
·REGAL CASTLE
5.0
Amazing!
So pretty!
Like a dream!
Best host EVER!
...AND SUCH GOOD REVIEWS, TOO!
AWOOOOOO
THOUGH IT DOES LOOK SOMEWHAT DIFFERENT IN THESE STORMY CIRCUMSTANCES...
BUT PENCILMATE ISN'T GOING TO LET A BIT OF BAD WEATHER AND SOME OVERENTHUSIASTIC WILDLIFE RUIN HIS TRIP.
GO BACK
TAXI
SCREECH!
THAT TAXI SURE WAS IN A HURRY, WHAT'S HIS DEAL?

OH WELL, HERE GOES NOTHING!
GET A LOAD OF THESE HAND-CARVED TRANSYLVANIAN DOORS. THEY DON'T MAKE 'EM LIKE THEY USED TO.
CREAK!!

LOOKS LIKE A SELF-SERVICE CHECK-IN. SURE IS NICE TO HAVE A BIT OF INDEPENDENCE! TRAVEL IS ABOUT ADVENTURE, AFTER ALL, NOT FREE GIFTS AND—
OOOH, FREE GIFTS?!
VELCOME GUEST
ALTHOUGH, THEY LOOK A BIT STALE...
MOON PASTE
STILL, YOU GOTTA GET YOUR MONEY'S WORTH.

How about a mint? The perfect thing to freshen your breath after a long journey.
...Definitely not a mint!
A local delicacy, maybe? Pencilmate loves foreign cuisine, but he's not very hungry right now. Perhaps later...
?
Finally, the host arrives! Time for the real pampering to commence.

AH, THE QUIET TYPE... SPLENDID! WHY CHITCHAT WHEN A PILLOW AWAITS!
GUEST Rooms ZIS VAY
THIS CUSTOMER SERVICE IS THE OPPOSITE OF HANDS-ON!
SNAP!

NOW, THIS IS A ROOM. BEAUTIFULLY APPOINTED, LUXURIOUSLY FURNISHED, VAPID NONSENSE WRITTEN ON THE WALLS. CLEARLY FIVE-STAR MATERIAL!
LIVE
LAUGH
LOVE
CHILLFLIX
NO ENTRY TO GUESTS
SLAM!
BUT IT APPEARS THERE'S BEEN A MISUNDERSTANDING.
NO ENTRY TO GUESTS

HERE'S PENCILMATE'S ROOM!
PERHAPS HE SHOULD'VE READ A FEW MORE REVIEWS...
?
PLOP!

COFFEE-MAKING FACILITIES.
AT LEAST THAT'S AS ADVERTISED.
NO, IT CAN'T BE!
JIMBO'S
COFFEE
DECAF
DECAF!?
TOSS
COFFEE
DOUBLE
DECAF
x2
DOUBLE DECAF!?

No...
No...
No...!
Is there any reasonable explanation for this oversight?
Disappointment levels . . . rising!
But surely his old friend television won't let him down?
Click
Out of batteries!
GASP!

WHERE'S THE EN SUITE HE WAS PROMISED?
En Suite
CALM DOWN, PENCILMATE. YOU'RE A CONSUMER. YOU KNOW YOUR RIGHTS.
TOWELS
NO TOWELS?! BUT THE LISTING SAID THERE'D BE TOWELS! WARM, MONOGRAMMED TOWELS!

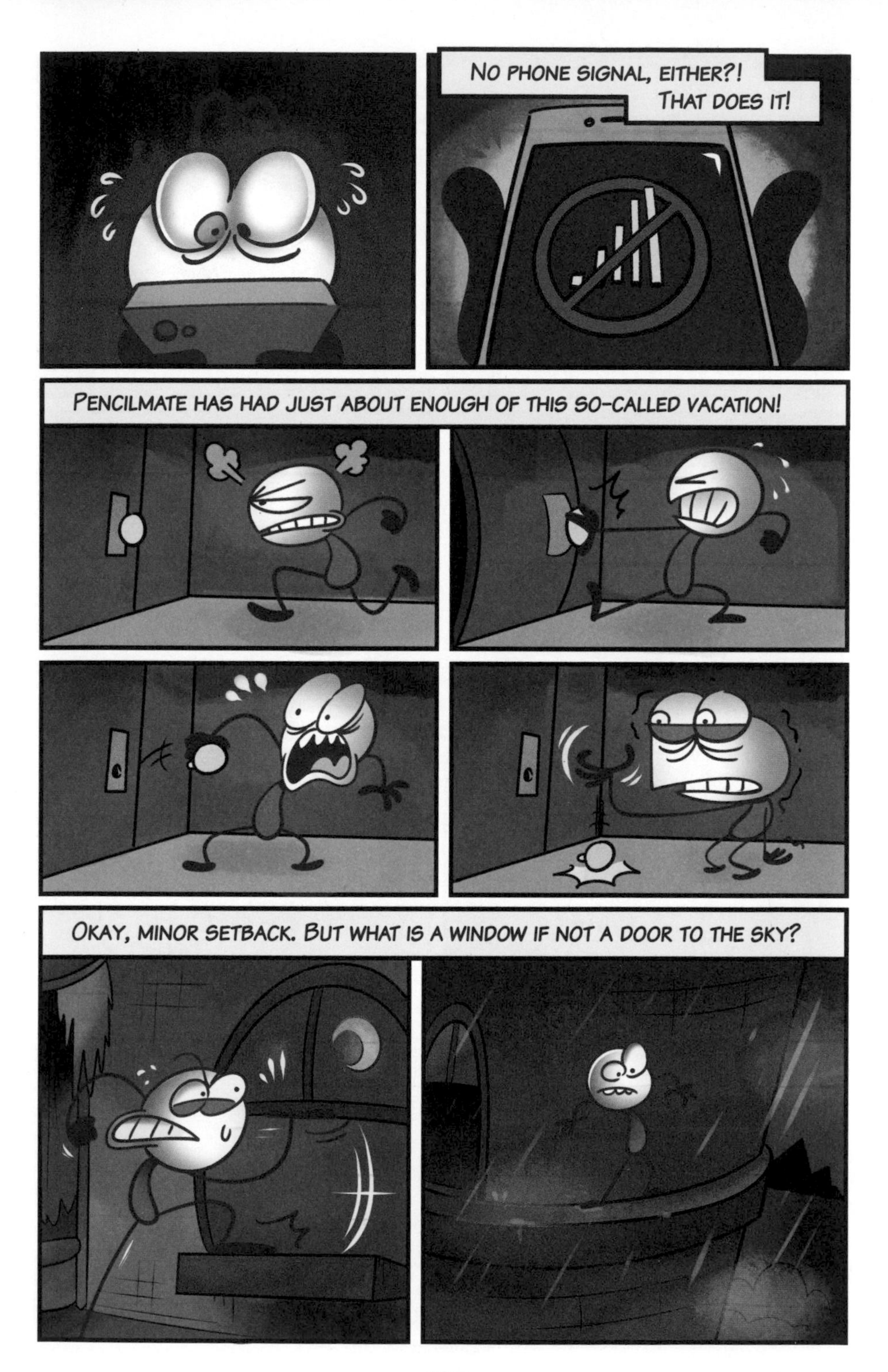
NO PHONE SIGNAL, EITHER?!
THAT DOES IT!
PENCILMATE HAS HAD JUST ABOUT ENOUGH OF THIS SO-CALLED VACATION!
OKAY, MINOR SETBACK. BUT WHAT IS A WINDOW IF NOT A DOOR TO THE SKY?

As he climbs, Pencilmate's anger only grows.
His first proper vacation in years, and this happens?
Out under the stars, Pencilmate has found one bar of signal! This is it!
Finally the time has come to really let this host know what he thinks of her listing.
REGAL CASTLE
No towel.
No batteries.
No caffeine.
VERY BAD HOST.
HEH...
HEH...
SEND
HEH...
Post that negative review, Pencilmate!

HA HA HA HA HA HA HA
SLIP!
BUT SLIPPERY FINGERS HAVE FAILED HIM AGAIN!
NOOOOOOOO
ZAP!!
AND THUS CONCLUDES PENCILMATE'S WORST VACATION EVER.
FIN

While it may appear to be nothing more than a simple geometric figure, the **Red Rhombus of Good Fortune** is an unimaginably powerful object infused with lucky cosmic energy, or something!

Just clip it out and slip it into your pocket for an immeasurably blessed day.

Don't believe us? Check out these 100% legitimate customer testimonials:

Don't be like Jerome!
Cut out your **Red Rhombus** and get lucky today!

RED RHOMBUS
OF GOOD FORTUNE!
BE SURE TO GET HELP FROM AN ADULT!

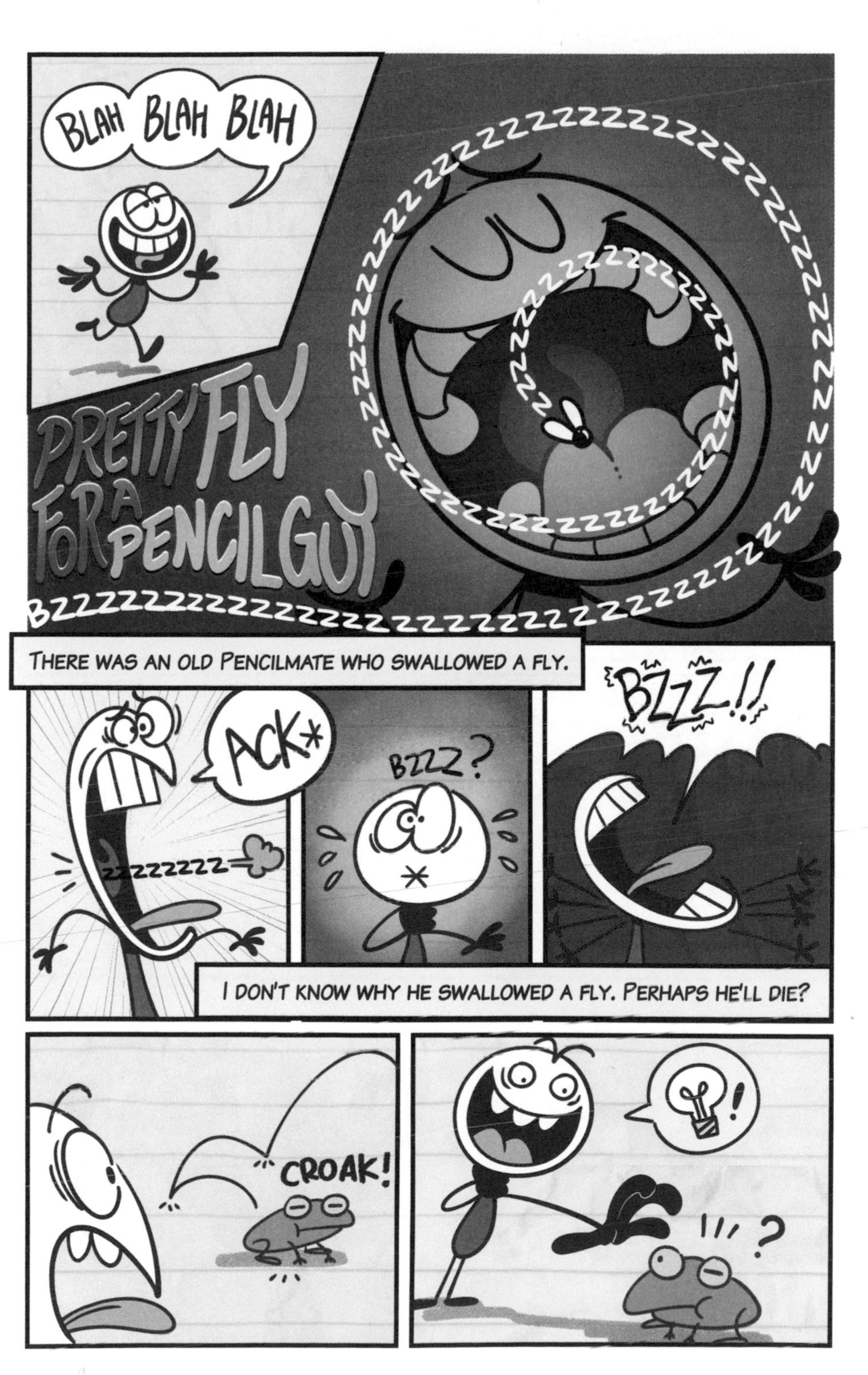
BLAH BLAH BLAH
PRETTY FLY FOR A PENCIL GUY
BZZZZZZZZZZZZZZZZZZZZZZZZZZZZZZ
THERE WAS AN OLD PENCILMATE WHO SWALLOWED A FLY.
ACK*
ZZZZZZZZ
BZZZ?
BZZZ!!
I DON'T KNOW WHY HE SWALLOWED A FLY. PERHAPS HE'LL DIE?
CROAK!
!
?

THERE WAS AN OLD PENCILMATE WHO SWALLOWED A FROG.
HE SWALLOWED A FROG TO CATCH THE FLY...
CROAK!
!!
SQUAWK
CROAK!
GULP!
HE SWALLOWED A SEAGULL TO CATCH THE FROG...
BUZZCROAKSQUAK

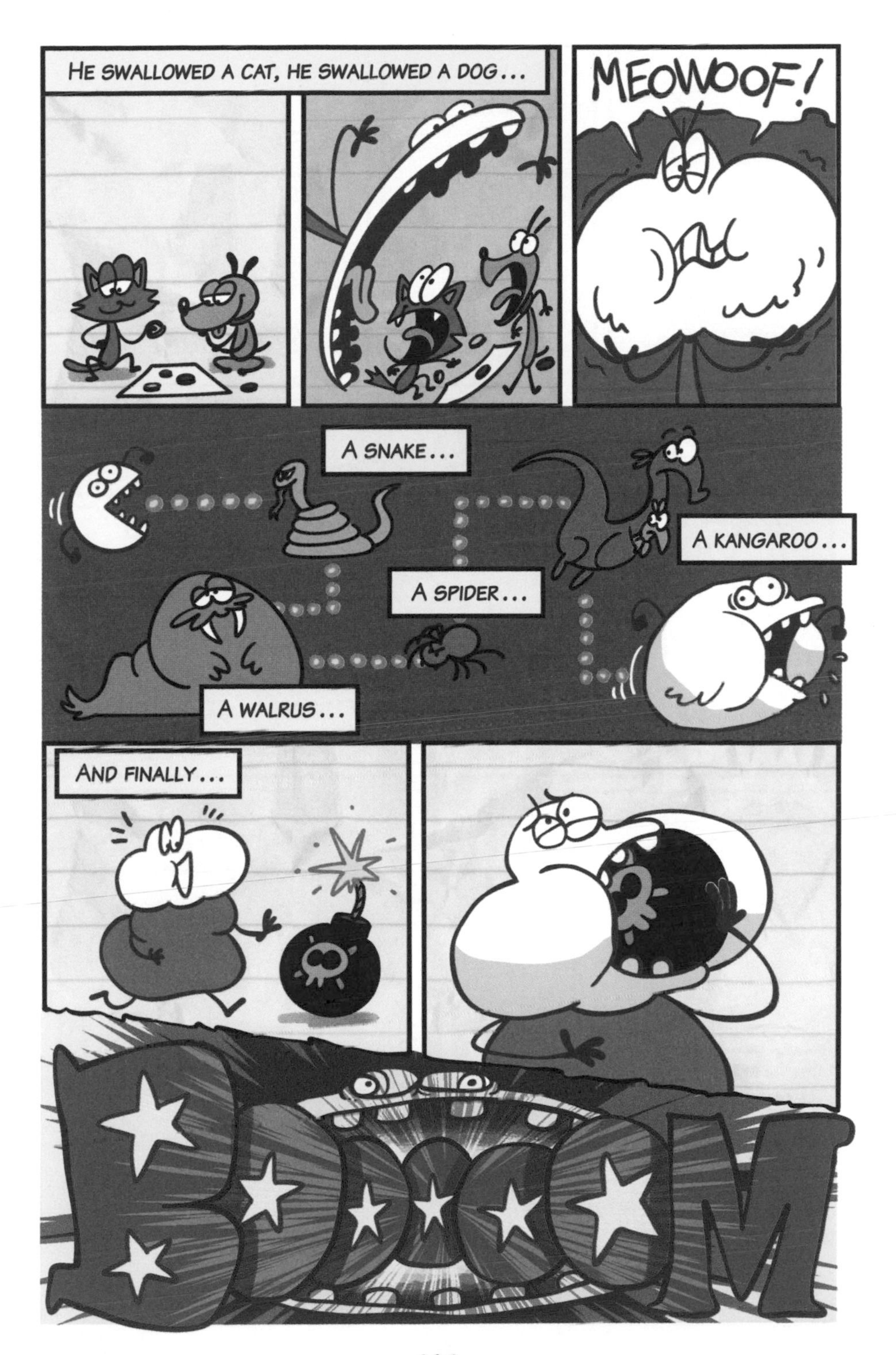
HE SWALLOWED A CAT, HE SWALLOWED A DOG...
MEOWOOF!
A SNAKE...
A KANGAROO...
A SPIDER...
A WALRUS...
AND FINALLY...
BOOM

G!#?@!
THERE WAS AN OLD FLY WHO SWALLOWED A PENCILMATE.
BLAH BLAH BLAH.
BLA...
END

The Fart Academy

Farts Gratia Fartis

Here at the ***Fart Academy,*** we believe that the backdoor breeze is more than a mere release of methane gas. A single fart can change the world, and with the correct academic guidance, you, too, can obtain the wind power to shape society's olfactory landscape.

THE UNMISTAKABLE STENCH of SUCCESS!

Toot your way to the top by learning countless advanced flatulatory skills, such as:

- Farting on Command
- Butthorn Music Theory
- Culinary Secrets to Cutting the Cheese
- Bum Chemistry, the Periodic Table, and You
- Bottom Burps to Win Friends and Influence People

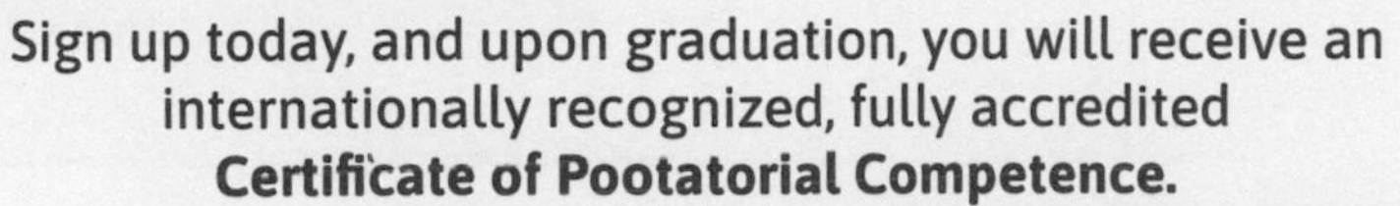

Sign up today, and upon graduation, you will receive an internationally recognized, fully accredited **Certificate of Pootatorial Competence.**

LIGHTS CAMOUFLAGE ACTION
AH! IT'S A BEAUTIFUL DAY!
THE SUN IS SHINING, THE BIRDS ARE CHIRPING, AND THERE IS A WHOLE FOREST FILLED WITH WOODLAND CREATURES...
JUST WAITING TO BE SHOT...
...BY A CAMERA!
THAT'S RIGHT, IT'S PHOTOGRAPHIN' SEASON! C'MERE, CRITTERS, AND GET YER PICTURE TOOK!
WOW, LOOK AT ALL THOSE GEESES, MEESES, AND ALBATREESES! COVER OF IRRATIONAL GEOGRAPHIC, HERE PENCILMATE COMES!

SUITED UP HEAD TO TOE IN CAMOUFLAGE, HE OUGHT TO BLEND IN PERFECTLY WITH HIS SURROUNDINGS!
NOW ALL HE NEEDS TO DO IS NOT MAKE A SINGLE—
SNAP!
SOUND.

HOLY STROMBOLI! THIS CAMO REALLY DOES THE TRICK!
WITH THIS OUTFIT, HE'S ESSENTIALLY INVISIBLE! LIKE VEGAN CHEESE DIP AT A POTLUCK...
BUT LOOKEE HERE! NATURE IS COMING TO HIM?! HOW WONDERFUL!
HOW MAGICAL!
OKAY, THIS IS A BIT MUCH.
AAAGGH! THIS IS JUST LIKE THAT HITCHCOCK MOVIE MARNIE!

After getting so flocked over, Pencilmate is relieved to find a calm place to catch his breath.
When suddenly to his surprise, an adorable little doe saunters in!
Also to his surprise, something less adorable saunters in!
This camo does its job too well! The hunter can't see Pencilmate!
And now he's square between a gun and its target!
CH-CHICK...
Ruh-roh!

RUMBLE
BEFORE THE HUNTER CAN GET HIS SHOT OFF, A LOUD RUMBLE COMES OUT OF THE NEARBY FOREST!
SAY, WHAT IS ALL THAT RACKET, ANYWAY?
ZIP
ZIP
AAAGGHHH!! IT'S A TREE MUNCHIN' MECHANICAL NIGHTMARE!!!
THE TREE MUNCHIN' MECHANICAL NIGHTMARE INC.

TARNATION! PENCILMATE'S CAMO IS MAKING HIM INVISIBLE AT THE WORST OF TIMES! NOW HE'S REALLY GOT TO MAKE LIKE A TREE—
AND LEAF!
DEFINITELY NOTHING HERE
TOO BAD HE'S SLOWER THAN A TORTOISE IN A TUB OF MOLASSES.
THIS LOOKS LIKE THE END FOR OUR ASPIRING PHOTOGRAPHER! CUT DOWN IN HIS PRIME! WHY, HE'S BARELY OLDER THAN A SAPLING!

RIIIPPP!
AHA! WHADDYA KNOW? THE MACHINE'S GONE AND RIPPED OFF ALL HIS CAMOUFLAGE, MAKING HIM SEEABLE AGAIN!
AND PERHAPS A LITTLE TOO, AHEM, AU NATUREL.
FLASH!
IRRATIONAL GEOGRAPHIC
WELL, I'LL BE! PENCILMATE'S MADE THE COVER OF *IRRATIONAL GEOGRAPHIC* AFTER ALL!
END

Pencilmiss is hooked on cheese,
it makes her go weak at the knees.
If it was a smaller vice,
there might be some left for the mice.

"Good night, good night to all the world!"
young Pencilmate yawned and said.
"Good night, good night right back at you!"
replied the beast beneath his bed.

Pencilmate felt there was a chance
he'd forgotten something for the dance.
He checked his tie,
and felt his fly,
then saw he was missing his pants!

Hooray, hooray, what happy fate!
A coin found in a sewer grate!
Pencilmate felt very lucky,
till he was flattened by a trucky.

A CYMBAL PLAN
???
!

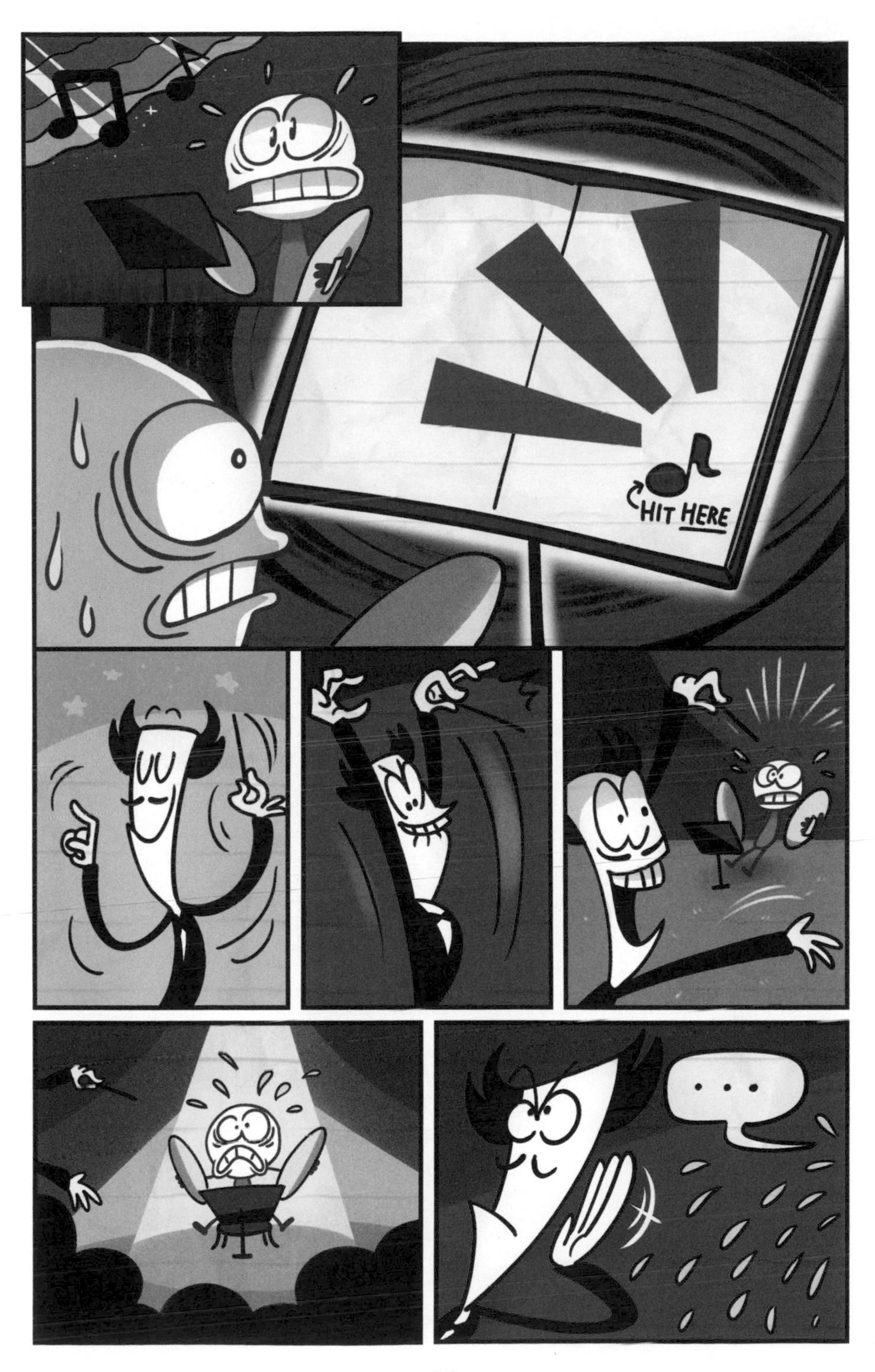
HIT HERE
...

YAAAAAAAY!!!
END

CREDITS

WRITTEN BY

Jared Woods, Andrew Martin,
Rachel Van Nes & Joe West

ROUGH SKETCHES

Andrew Howell, Ridge Idzikowski,
Yuri Custodio Peroba & Hamid Borzooey

LINE ART

Sangsoo Kim, Josh Floyd & Yunkyung Kim

COLOR PALETTE

Sangsoo Kim, Neil Kohney,
Ridge Idzikowski & Dane Georges

COVER CONCEPT

Andrew Howell

COVER ILLUSTRATION

Neil Kohney

BOOK DESIGN

Taylor Abatiell

ADDITIONAL ILLUSTRATIONS

Neil Kohney

PRODUCTION COORDINATORS

Cat Pandiani & Greg Pearce

TALENT COORDINATOR

Cameron Jones

SPECIAL THANKS TO THE ENTIRE PENCILMATION CAST AND CREW!